The House in Norham Gardens

Also by Penelope Lively

Astercote
The Driftway
Fanny and the Monsters
The Ghose of Thomas Kempe
Going Back
The Revenge of Samuel Stokes
A Stitch in Time
The Voyage of QV66
The Whispering Knights
The Wild Hunt of Hagworthy

for younger readers

Dragon Trouble

Penelope Lively

The House in Norham Gardens

Mammoth

'Old Furniture' by Thomas Hardy, from
Collected Poems, is reprinted by permission
of the trustees of the Hardy Estate,
the Macmillan Company of Canada and
Macmillan, London and Basingstoke

First published in Great Britain 1974
by Heinemann Young Books
Published 1994 by Mammoth
Reissued 1999 by Mammoth
an imprint of Egmont Children's Books Limited
239 Kensington High Street, London W8 6SA

Text copyright © Penelope Lively, 1974
Cover illustration copyright © Sarah Perkins, 1999

The moral rights of the author and
cover illustrator have been asserted.

ISBN 0 7497 0790 9

10 9 8 7 6 5 4 3 2 1

A CIP catalogue record for this title
is available from the British Library

Printed and bound in Great Britain
by Cox & Wyman Ltd, Reading, Berkshire

To my mother

I know not how it may be with others
  Who sit amid relics of householdry
That date from the days of their mothers' mothers,
  But well I know how it is with me
    Continually.

I see the hands of the generations
  That owned each shiny familiar thing
In play on its knobs and indentations,
  And with its ancient 'fashioning
    Still dallying:

Hands behind hands, growing paler and paler,
  As in a mirror a candle-flame
Shows images of itself, each frailer
  As it recedes, though the eye may frame
    Its shape the same.

'Old Furniture'—Thomas Hardy

CHAPTER 1

There is an island. At the heart of the island there is a valley. In the valley, among blue mountains, a man kneels before a piece of wood. He paints on it—sometimes with a fibre brush, sometimes with his finger. The man himself is painted: bright dyes—red, yellow, black—on brown skin. He wears pearshell, green beetles in his hair, and a bunch of tangket leaves. The year is 1900: in England Victoria is queen. The man is remote from England in distance by half the circumference of the world: in understanding, by five thousand years.

Belbroughton Road. Linton Road. Bardwell Road. The houses there are quite normal. They are ordinary sizes and have ordinary chimneys and roofs and gardens with laburnum and flowering cherry. Park Town. As you go south they are growing. Getting higher and odder. By the time you get to Norham Gardens they have tottered over the edge into madness: these are not houses but flights of fancy. They are three stories high and disguise themselves as churches. They have ecclesiastical porches instead of front doors and round norman windows or pointed gothic ones, neatly grouped in threes with flaring brick to set them off. They reek of hymns and the Empire, Mafeking and the Khyber Pass, Mr Gladstone and Our Dear Queen. They have nineteen rooms and half a dozen chimneys and iron fire escapes. A bomb couldn't blow them up, and the privet in their gardens has survived two World Wars.

People live in these houses. Clare Mayfield, aged fourteen, raised by aunts in North Oxford.

Clare came round the corner out of Banbury Road and the history books and maths things and *Jane Eyre* in her bicycle basket lurched over to one side with the string bag of shopping, and unbalanced her. She got off and straightened them and then pedalled fast, standing up, past the ranks of parked cars and the flurry of students coming out of the language school on the corner. She swung into the half-moon of weedy gravel that was the front drive of number forty Norham Gardens, and put the bike into the shed at the side of the house. Wind, cold January wind, funnelled up the chasm between number forty and the house next door, clutching her bare legs and rattling the dustbin lid. Clare stuffed the books on top of the shopping in the string bag and went up the front steps, quickly.

The front door was not locked. Old ladies lose front door keys. Clare went across the hall and through the green baize swing door into the kitchen. The house was silent. Silence reached away up to the top of the house, up the well of the staircase past the first floor and up to the attic rooms, spiced only by the ticking of clocks: the kitchen one, loudly insensitive, the grandfather clock on the stairs, discreetly chiming since before the Boer War, Maureen's Smith Alarm-o-matic, marking time by itself up there under the roof. Maureen would not be back for another hour or so. And the aunts —the aunts would be in the library, dozing quietly beside a fire that they would have forgotten to keep stoked. They were always in the library at half-past four. They migrated slowly through the house during the day: from their bedrooms to the breakfast-room to the study to the dining-room. I am the only person I know, Clare thought, who has a special room for having breakfast in. And a pantry and a flower-room and a silver cupboard and a scullery and three lavatories. She put the kettle on and had a conversation in her head with a person from outer space who was ignorant of these things. A flower-room, she said severely, is for arranging flowers in. A long time ago ladies who hadn't got anything much to do did that in the mornings. My great-grandmother, for instance. My aunts, on the other hand, never arranged flowers. They were a different kind of person. They always had things to do. They wrote articles and translated Anglo-Saxon and sat on committees.

They are not ordinary aunts.

The kettle began to mutter to itself. Clare unpacked the string bag and saw that there was a note from Mrs Hedges. 'I put a steak and kidney in the oven for your supper, and I want it eaten, mind. See your Aunt Anne remembers her pills. The coal come and I paid him but it's gone up again. We owe the milkman one fifty.'

Three cups on a tray. Crown Derby. Very valuable. One cracked, one with an odd saucer. Would the milkman like one cracked Crown Derby cup instead of one pound fifty pence. Probably not. A situation when milkmen and coal men and electricity men are asking you for more money than you have got to give them is called a financial problem, in posh language. In simpler terms it is a gap on a piece of paper between what you have got and what people want you to pay them. Most people of fourteen are not bothered about that kind of thing. If, however, you live with your aunts and your aunts are around eighty years old and not very good at working things out or knowing how much things cost, though very good indeed in all sorts of other ways, then you have to be bothered. You have to fill the gap somehow.

The gap, in this instance, had been filled with Maureen.

'A lodger!' Mrs Hedges had said. 'They'd never hear of a lodger!' That had been a month ago now, when she and Mrs Hedges had sat one each side of the kitchen table and considered things. The Outgoings and the Assets, and the cracked guttering that must be repaired and the leaking kitchen sink that would have to be replaced.

'I'd mention it to them,' said Mrs Hedges. 'But you don't want to fuss them, at their age, and they've not really got the hang of decimals, have they?'

And so it had all been laid on the table, as it were.

'Mmm,' said Mrs Hedges. 'Sure there's nothing else? Just their pensions and your little bit from when your mum and dad—from this legacy?'

'Nothing else.'

'No Securities? They'd have Securities, people like your aunts. Shares and that.'

'No. Not now. There were some, but the Bank Manager wrote

last year and said he was sorry but they'd got smaller and smaller until they'd kind of disappeared. There was three pounds fifty pence left.'

'Shame,' said Mrs Hedges. 'Were they upset—the old ladies?'

'No. They've never been particularly interested in money.'

'They've not had to be. And they're a bit vague, now they're getting on, so it's up to us, not that I'd want anyone to be thinking me sticking my nose into what's not my business.'

'Anyone isn't thinking anything like that,' said Clare.

'Right, then,' said Mrs Hedges. 'Let's look at these Outgoings and see what we can cut down on.'

'Food. I could keep a cow in the garden. Grow vegetables.'

Mrs Hedges glared. 'I'm not laughing. You don't eat properly, as it is, any of you. All those tins.'

'They don't notice what they eat.'

'But you're a growing girl. Food's got to stay as it is. Clothes?'

'Jumble sales.'

'Another year or two and you're going to want stuff like the other girls have, from boutiques and that. Fashionable stuff.'

'There's trunks of their old things upstairs,' said Clare. 'Long velvet skirts and floppy hats. Dead smart nowadays. I'll be terribly grand.'

'Get away with you. Holidays?'

'My cousins in Norfolk. That's free.'

'I'm an outgoing,' said Mrs Hedges. 'But you can't keep this place clean on your own, that's for sure.'

'So we can't cut down on you. Good.'

'Rates. That we can't do anything about. It's a mercy there's no rent to think of. They do own this house, don't they?'

'It's something called a Lease.'

'Ah,' said Mrs Hedges. 'Them. How long's it got to go?'

'Fifteen years, then it isn't their house any more.'

'Well, we won't worry beyond that.'

'Why not?' said Clare coldly. Aunt Anne is seventy-eight and Aunt Susan is eighty. She had looked away from Mrs Hedges and out of the steamy window to the coalshed and the dank brick wall and the cat prowling in the privet and the kitchen clock had

4

ticked, loud and stupid. And Mrs Hedges had got all busy totting up the figures again and talking about Assets.

'Assets?'

'What have you *got*?'

'A house with nineteen rooms.'

The house squatted around them, vast, empty, unnecessary and indestructible. You had to be a fat busy Victorian family to expand enough to fill up basements and passages and conservatories and attics. You had to have an army of bootboys and nurses and parlour-maids. You had to have a complicated, greedy system of living that used up plenty of space and people just in the daily business of eating and sleeping and keeping clean. You had to multiply your requirements and your possessions, activate that panel of bells in the kitchen—Drawing-Room and Master Bedroom and Library—keep going a spiral of needs and people to satisfy the needs. If you did not, if you contracted into three people without such needs, then a house like this became a dinosaur, occupying too much air and ground and demanding to be fed new sinks and drainpipes and a sea of electricity. Such a house became a fossil, stranded among neighbours long since chopped up into flats and bed-sitting-rooms, or sleek modern houses that had a suitable number of rooms for correct living in the late twentieth century. It, and its kind, stood awkwardly on the fringes of a city renowned for old and beautiful buildings: they were old, and unbeautiful.

Perhaps, Clare thought, you should knock down places like this when they are no longer useful. Reduce them to the brick and dust from which they came?

Or should you, just because they are old, not beautiful, but old, keep them? Houses like this have stood and watched the processes of change. People swept by the current, go with it: they grow, learn, forget, laugh and cry, replace their skin every seven years, lose teeth, form opinions, become bald, love, hate, argue and reflect. Bricks, roofs, windows and doors are immutable. Before them have passed carriages, and the carriages have given way to bicycles and the bicycles to the cars that line up now, bumper to shining bumper, along the pavement. In front of them have paraded ankle-length dresses and boaters and frock coats and plus-fours and duffle coats

5

and mini skirts. Through their doors have passed heads, shingled, bobbed, permed and unkempt. Within their walls language has changed, and assumptions, and the furniture of people's minds. Possibly, just possibly, you must keep the shells inside which such things happen, in case you forget about the things themselves.

'That's twelve rooms more than you need,' said Mrs Hedges. 'One way and another.'

And at that point had flowered in Clare's mind the notion that if you had more rooms than you in fact needed there were, by the same token, and according to the convenient arrangement of supply and demand, people who needed rooms.

'They'd never hear of a lodger!' Mrs Hedges had declared. 'Not in a month of Sundays.' And she had been entirely wrong. She had not reckoned with the aunts' ability to review a situation. They, unlike the house, had not set hard in 1890. They had evolved with the century, taking on the protective colouring of different years, but without sacrificing personalities more forceful than the ebb and flow of opinion. All their lives they had examined the times, decided what was sound, and discarded what was not. Fashion they ignored: the fascination of change sustained them. And it was perfectly sound, they at once declared, that there should be a lodger at Norham Gardens if circumstances required it.

And from that decision, to the arrival of Maureen with two tartan suitcases and some brown paper parcels, had been a short route by way of a postcard in the window of the shop in North Parade.

Clare added digestive biscuits to the Crown Derby cups on the tray, the teapot, bread and peanut butter for herself, and Aunt Anne's pills. Then she went through into the hall, bumping backwards through the swing door and balancing the tray against her arm while she opened the library door.

It was twilight in the library, partly because the January afternoon light had almost all leaked away by now, and partly because it was always half dark in there. The windows were curtained floor to ceiling in toffee-brown velvet: beyond them the garden stretched away bleakly to the wall at the end, the long grass flattened and ribbed with snow that had melted and then frozen again. Clare drew the curtains and turned on the light. Now it was almost cosy. There were books instead of walls—in bookcases as long as the bookcases lasted and then overflowing into piles and toppling columns. There were stacks of box-files, too, labelled long ago with dusty labels on which the ink had faded into obscurity, like invisible writing that refuses to be reanimated. And there were great mountains of paper, yellowing articles with titles like 'Kinship Structure among the Baganda'. And spears. Clare, putting the tray down on the table by the sofa, thought: I am also the only person I know who has spears on their walls instead of pictures. Arranged in a nice pattern.

A further thought struck her. 'Can I borrow some of the spears for *Macbeth*?'

The aunts were sitting on either side of the fire, in the leather arm-chairs that leaked tufts of some strange stuffing on to the carpet. They had been dozing, probably, and sat up now with a start, as though guilty.

Aunt Susan said, 'By all means. But they would not be at all authentic, you know. They come from Basutoland, not Scotland.'

'We're not that fussy. Thanks.'

Aunt Anne said, 'I hope they are not the ones with poisoned tips.' They studied the fan of spears for a moment, anxiously.

'No,' said Aunt Susan. 'Those went to the Pitt Rivers in 1939. I remember now.'

Clare picked up the shovel and put some more coal on the fire. She poked it and sparks showered away into the dark chimney. She kissed Aunt Susan and then Aunt Anne. Their faces felt soft and papery, like tissues. Their hair, seen in close-up, was thin and fine like a young child's, Aunt Susan's white and wavy, Aunt Anne's brown peppered with grey, pulled back into a knot behind her head. They had on their brown tweed suits, made by the tailor in Walton Street before the last war, and fur-lined boots. It was never really warm in the library, just a localised warmth around the fire.

'Had a good day, dear?'

'It was all right. We've got to decide about O levels. German, or Physics and Chem.'

The aunts looked at each other, and then at Clare, their faces puckered with incomprehension.

'Exams,' said Clare. 'I think I'll do Physics and Chem.'

The aunts brightened. They knew all about exams.

'Very sensible,' said Aunt Susan. 'A good grounding in the Sciences is right for a girl. Nowadays. Tea, dear?'

Aunt Susan's hand was oddly small now. It shook a little; the cup jigged in the saucer. They had shrunk, the aunts. People do that when they get old. In photographs of fifteen, twenty years ago they were taller by nine inches or a foot.

'But Clare will be on the arts side,' said Aunt Anne. 'Surely. History or English.'

'Nevertheless. For the mental discipline.'

'You may be right. But I see her as History. Or the Social Sciences.'

They looked at Clare with love and pride. Much was expected.

'Somerville, I think. Or Lady Margaret Hall.'

'The new Universities are well thought of now, I understand.'

Clare said, 'I don't expect they'll want me.' She put three lumps of sugar in her tea, and spread the peanut butter thick. You need sustaining, in January in the South Midlands when you've biked back from school with the wind against you and cars spraying slush up your bare legs.

The aunts smiled, disbelievingly.

'Or I might leave school at fifteen and work in a boutique.'

'A boutique?'

'A kind of shop with pop songs coming out of the walls. Don't worry. Joke.'

'She is teasing us,' said Aunt Susan.

'Taking advantage of our infirmities.'

They beamed.

'That's right,' said Clare. 'Seriously, though, I think I'll be a pop star. Then I can buy us all fur coats.'

'She means,' said Aunt Anne, 'a popular singer.'

Aunt Susan said, 'I am well aware of that. No doubt she would be surprised to learn that we've heard of pop art, too. Pictures of film actresses, repeated many times.'

'And tins of soup, perfectly reproduced.'

You never knew with the aunts. 'B double plus,' said Clare. 'Good, conscientious work. A maxi coat?'

'A garment to the ankles. That could be deduced semantically.'

'B plus. A discotheque?'

'An establishment selling gramophone records?'

'B minus. Write out corrections three times. A milk-bar?'

'A brand of confectionary.'

'C minus. See me in break.'

'Our turn,' said Aunt Susan. 'Who succeeded Lloyd George as Prime Minister?'

'I've forgotten just at the moment.'

'Gamma plus. The terms of the Munich Agreement?'

'I think I'll clear the tea and get on with my French homework,' said Clare. 'Match drawn.'

'Grimbly Hughes sent the wrong digestives,' said Aunt Anne. 'I'll pop down there tomorrow and have a word with Mr Fisher.'

Clare said, 'No, you won't. I'll do it. The roads are all icy.' Old ladies can slip on icy roads, and fall down. Anyway, it isn't Grimbly Hughes, it's the supermarket in Summertown. Grimbly Hughes hasn't existed for fifteen years, Mrs Hedges says.

'We put too much on her,' said Aunt Susan. 'She's too young to be bothered about grocers.'

They were concerned now: concerned, and cross with themselves.

'One is so incompetent, at our age.'

'Such a nuisance. Useless. I could take my stick, Clare, and go very slowly.'

'No,' said Clare. 'Anyway, think what good practice it is. For when I get married. If I get married. I'll know all about buying biscuits and ordering coal and having gutters mended. There is one thing, though. Could you help me with my Latin translation later, Aunt Anne?'

Aunt Anne glowed, useful again.

If I get married. P'raps I won't. P'raps I'll be busy instead, like the aunts. Except I'm not as bright as the aunts were. Are.

The aunts had not married. They had gone to university in the days when girls stayed at home to help their mothers or made a suitable match. There were pictures of them upstairs in the drawing-room, pretty and plump and determined in long black skirts and tight waists and leg-of-mutton sleeves and black caps and gowns. They'd got degrees and then more degrees and then they'd settled down in Norham Gardens and taught undergraduates from their old college and sallied forth to London every now and then to sit on Committees or take part in Enquiries. They wrote indignant letters to *The Times* and joined in protest marches and when the war came they fire-watched and took in evacuees. There had never been time for marriage.

Clare left the aunts in the library. They would sit there till suppertime now, reading and dozing, according to the pattern of their day. Now that they were old their lives had contracted. The house, which had always been their base, had become also their shell. It held everything they needed and they seldom went beyond it. The outside world came to them through newspapers and the windows and Clare and Mrs Hedges and they received it with interest but no longer tried to influence it. 'We have been useful in our time,' said Aunt Susan. 'Now it's our turn to sit and watch.'

In the kitchen, Clare put the tea-things away and got her books out. It was slightly warmer than usual because the oven was on with Mrs Hedges' pie in it, so she pulled a chair up and sat with her feet against the oven door, learning French verbs. The kitchen clock ticked and the pipes made the asthmatic wheezes and gurgles they always made, and water dripped from the crack in the sink into the bucket you had to remember to keep standing underneath. Outside, the evening thickened and darkened and became night. Down in the middle of Oxford bells rang. Cars came and went in Crick Road and Norham Gardens and their headlights sent yellow patches up the kitchen wall and across the ceiling and down the other wall.

The front door clicked open and slammed shut again. Then Maureen's head came round the baize door.

'Hello. It's perishing out, let me tell you. By the way, I could do with another blanket.'

Clare said, 'I'll get one. There's some in the chest in the junk-room, I think.'

They went upstairs together, Maureen talking loudly of her day. She worked in an estate-agent's office. Clare knew all about the life of the office, Maureen's views of the boss and the junior partner and the new young fellow who'd come last week and the girls all thought he was dishy but Maureen didn't fancy him, personally. Maureen was twenty-eight. She trailed an atmosphere of vague dissatisfaction, of undefined emotions which sometimes homed on such personal failures as her hair, which she thought too wavy, and her weight, which was apparently seven pounds above what was correct for her age and height. She was extremely kind.

'Which is the junk-room, then?' said Maureen. 'Honestly, it's a proper rabbit warren, this place.'

'It's the attic room next to yours,' said Clare. They climbed the last flight. 'Third floor, Ladies Outfitting and Restaurant,' said Maureen. 'One thing, I'll lose a pound or two going up and down here every day.'

Before Maureen's inspection visit, Mrs Hedges and Clare had been worried about her possible reaction to Norham Gardens. As Mrs Hedges said, things were not exactly up-to-date. They need not have bothered. She had tried everything out in a methodical way, bouncing on the bed and poking the pillow and sitting down in the arm-chair. She pulled a face at the gas-fire, which had been there since about 1940 and was that kind with crumbling columns of stuff like grey icing-sugar. The gas-ring wasn't much better, but the electric kettle was newish.

'Bathroom?'

'It's on the floor underneath,' Clare had said. 'But there's a lavatory next door.'

They inspected the lavatory. Maureen giggled. Then she said, 'Sorry, dear, but it is a bit of a museum-piece, isn't it?'

Some of us prefer our lavatories in brown mahogany with the bowl encircled in purple flowers and a cistern called 'The Great Niagara'.

But the lavatory had not proved a serious obstacle. After looking round the room once more Maureen had said delicately, 'Are there any other—guests?'

'No. You'd be the only one.'

'Three fifty, you said?'

'Yes.'

'Front door key?'

'Yes. If I can find one.'

'I'll take it. I don't mind telling you, I thought there'd be a snag. I said to myself, if it's only three fifty then that means the toilet's outside or there's foreign girl students two to a room in the rest of the house and wirelesses blaring till all hours. I've seen some funny places, I can tell you, room-hunting.'

And Clare had said, 'Oh, have you?' relieved.

They went into the junk-room together, Clare groping for the light. These rooms on the top floor were the ones with the most ecclesiastical windows of all, bunched together in triplicate like those high above the central aisle of a church. The ones at the front squinted right over to the University Parks and the Clarendon Laboratory and University Museum. Maureen thought the outlook distinguished: it made you think, she said, looking at all that and knowing there's all those characters inside there getting on with whatever it is they get on with.

Clare found the light and the room came to life, trunks piled on top of one another, the shape of chairs looming under tattered dust-sheets, the ancient sewing-machine with its wheels and treadles looking like a blueprint for the industrial revolution, the huge tulip-mouth of the gramophone's loudspeaker, flowered china jugs and matching basins, a dressmaker's dummy, trouser presses, hat boxes . . .

'Good grief!' said Maureen. 'They don't believe in throwing things away, the old ladies, do they?'

'If you keep things you can go on being sure about what's happened to you.'

Maureen said doubtfully, 'I suppose that's one way of looking at it.'

Clare began opening trunks. Most of them were full of old clothes. Great-grandmother's for the most part, elaborate construc-

tions of silk, lace and whalebone. Maureen stared in amazement.
'Well! I wouldn't have thought they'd have been that dressy, your aunts.'

'These aren't their things—they belonged to great-grandmother. Their mother.'

'They're your great-aunts really, then?'

'Yes.'

'Stands to reason, of course. I hadn't been thinking.'

Clare heaved the top trunk down and tried the next. Maureen, fiddling with the handle of the gramophone, said, 'Have you always lived with them?'

'Since I was eight.'

There was a pause. Wrong trunk, again: this one was full of hats. Maureen said, 'What happened to, er . . . ?'

'There was this accident. They had to go in aeroplanes a lot, because of my father's job.'

'I see,' said Maureen, looking hard at the loudspeaker. Then she added, 'Shame.'

'I think the blankets are in this one. Could you help me lift off the one on top?'

It was a vast leather-buckled trunk with tattered labels on it that said 'P & O Line. Not Wanted on Voyage'. Across the lid of the trunk was scrawled, in white chalk 'Sydney to London'. They took one end each, to lift it down, and the hinges promptly burst off, bringing the lid with them. In no other house, thought Clare, in absolutely no other house, could you open an old trunk and be confronted with a large bundle of bows and arrows. And what looked like a set of very moth-eaten feather dusters and a lot of old coconut matting and a weird-looking slab of wood with some kind of a picture on it. 'Good grief!' said Maureen again.

Clare shook out one of the feather dusters and it became a head-dress, the colours all faded. A bit smelly. She picked one of the bows up, twanged it, and aimed an arrow towards the window.

'Do you think I could get the next-door cat, if I aimed very carefully?'

'Put it down, for goodness' sake,' said Maureen. 'You don't know where it's been. What are they, anyway?'

13

'They'll be something to do with my great-grandfather,' said Clare. 'He was an anthropologist. He went to queer places and brought things back.'

Maureen peered into the trunk with distaste. 'You can say that again.'

'He gave tons of things to the Pitt Rivers Museum. Have you ever been there? I expect these things were meant for there and got forgotten.'

'Well, fancy ... You mean they'd wear those things on their heads, the natives?'

'Mmn. There's photos somewhere, that he took. In the drawing-room desk.'

'And what would they have on otherwise?'

'Just paint. In stripes.'

'Well!' said Maureen. 'Rather you than me! Here, put the lid back on, I should think there'd be no end of germs and things in with that lot.'

Clare said, 'Hang on a moment ...' She picked up the slab of wood, and stared at it. It was about three feet long, and roughly oval, but wider at the top than the bottom. And painted; black, red and yellow, but the colours were dimmed now with dirt, and faded. One had the feeling that once they had been sharp and bright. It had a head, this thing, and a body, but so stylised that perhaps it was just a pattern, a pattern of swooping lines and jagged decoration like fish-hooks or zig-zag edging, loops and swirls. But on the other hand perhaps it was not a pattern, and if it was not then the head had eyes, huge and blank, and a gaping mouth.

'That gives me the creeps,' said Maureen. 'It's nasty. Put it back, do.'

'Just a minute.' It was a painting, but it was also a carving, because the lines had been gouged into the wood before they were painted. It seemed to say something: if you understood its language, if this kind of thing, this picture, this pattern, was a language, then it must have been a shout, once, to someone. Now, up here in the attic, to them, it was a whisper, a whisper you couldn't even understand.

They closed the trunk up again, and found the blankets in the one underneath, and Clare left the slab of wood, the shield or whatever it was, standing upright against the old sewing-machine because for some obscure reason it seemed wrong to bury it in the trunk again. And it stood there staring with those round owl-eyes out into the night where sleet was spearing down from a purple sky, glinting in the flares of light from the street lamps.

Maureen went to her room to make cocoa on the gas-ring and write to her mother in Weybridge. Clare sat with the aunts in the library, where Aunt Susan read *The Times* and Aunt Anne wrote letters, to an old friend, to the cousins in Norfolk, and to someone she taught, once, a long time ago. Clare stared at the fire for a bit, enjoying the red caverns and grottoes, and then got tired of that and looked round for a book. That was something you could never run short of in this house. Mrs Hedges must have been doing some tidying—some stray columns of books had been re-arranged on to a window shelf, revealing a small bookcase Clare couldn't remember having seen before. It was presumably great-grandfather's, for the books were old, with that distinctive, by no means unpleasant smell peculiar to books published before about 1930. They had titles like *Travels in Uzbekhistan*, *Headhunters of Brazil*, and *The Watutsi of the Sudan: A Study*. She picked out one called *New Guinea: the Unknown Island*, partly because it had some pictures, and took it over to the fire to read.

Outside, snow fell on North Oxford: on the Parks and the river and the old, dark laurel in the gardens and the brick and iron of the big houses. It drove people off the streets, and later a wind got up and rattled the bare trees. A cat yowled among the dustbins in Bradmore Road.

CHAPTER 2

The tamburan is finished. It stands now in the men's house, its meaning secret and complex, its circled eyes of red dye staring past the bamboo and the casuarina trees towards the mountains. The valley is quiet now, at midday. The women are working in the gardens, using digging sticks. The men rest. They talk, and sleep, and sharpen stone adzes on a rock. They have no past: no history. The future is tomorrow, and perhaps the next day. There is no word for love in their language, but they mourn their dead and remember their ancestors. Their world is peopled with the ghosts of their tribe, and they live with spirits as easily as with tree and mountain and river. Their world is two-faced: what seems to be and what lies beyond appearance. A stone is a stone and a tree is a tree—but they are also the qualities of stones and trees and must be approached in a certain way. Objects, too, have spirits.

Clare stood at her window and saw that the snow had all gone. Indeed, it was hot and sunny outside and the grass, intensely green, had grown until it was two or three feet high. There was a clamour of birds: twitterings, song, and occasional harsh shrieks that recalled the aviary at London Zoo. There was a path down the centre of the garden, a parting in the grass, and the brick wall at the end had disappeared. At the same moment as she noticed this, she found herself down there, in the garden, with the sensation of having either jumped or flown, and knew also that she was dreaming. Both house and garden had gone now, and the other houses. Instead, there was a complex green landscape of trees and undergrowth above which lifted, some way away, mountainous horizons, blue peaks soaring to heights lost among thick clouds.

It was beautiful, with the impersonal, unreal beauty of a poster in a travel agents'. There were large iridescent butterflies feeding among flowers at the edge of the path, and other insects. Stooping, she found herself staring at an immense spider hunched among stalks of grass. It was dark brown, both hairy and glistening at the same time. Repelled, she walked on. There was a feeling of detachment about the landscape, as though it were suspended in some way. It was impossible to know what time of day it might be—early or late—and it did not occur to her to look for the sun though she felt its warmth on her arms and face. She had a vague feeling of obligation, as if she were here for a purpose, and this kept her moving steadily along the path.

Presently a new sound interrupted the bird-noises, and there was a smell of bonfires. She realised that there were people ahead, concealed by the tall plants with long flat leaves that grew at either side of the path. Rounding a corner, she came upon them quite suddenly, in a clearing where there were low round huts, thatched, and open fires. Small, dark people they were, and there were children, squatting in the dust, and pig-like animals, and dogs. She felt uneasy now, but interested at the same time, and remembered that all she had to do, if anything unpleasant seemed about to happen, was to wake herself up.

She walked towards the people. They looked up and saw her, and began to chatter among themselves, watching her. Two or three of the men, who had been sitting by their fires, eating, stood up. She stopped, and one of the men moved towards her, gesturing. It was hard to know if he was threatening her or not, but something about his face alarmed her, now, and so, by a deliberate effort of will, she woke herself. There was a sensation of surging upward, through fathomless seas, which lasted for no time at all, and she was in her own bed, awake, and the clock said twenty past two. She turned over and slept till morning, by which time the dream had lost any precision. She remembered only that she had had a dream in which she had known she was dreaming.

The snow that had fallen in the night melted a little and then froze again during an afternoon that ended even before the last lesson at school, with darkness clamping down at four. Clare cycled home through grey twilight spiked with car headlights. Somewhere outside, beyond the houses and streets, there would be a Christmas-card world of white fields and woods lying dapper in a still night, but in North Oxford the snow had turned to brown and grey and people hurried past with their heads down against the cold. The big houses brooded behind curtained windows, facing each other in stolid ranks.

Clare stopped in North Parade for tins of soup, and bread. When she got back to the house Mrs Rider from next door was banging snow and slush into the gutter with a broom.

'Hallo. I did your bit too, while I was about it.'

'Thanks,' said Clare.

Mrs Rider was a landlady. Her house swarmed with students. There were bicycle racks outside and typed notices in the hall about Rules and Wirelesses in Bedrooms and Use of Bathrooms. The house was a twin of number forty, but disembowelled. It had lost its panels of bells, its scullery and flower-room and silver cupboard. Instead there were bed-sitting-rooms with built-in cupboards, central heating, bathrooms on every floor. Only its outside remembered. A posse of students came down the steps, chattering and be-scarved, American, French, Chinese.

Mrs Rider said, 'The old ladies keeping well, are they? I've not seen them about lately.'

'They're all right. Aunt Anne's got a bad chest so she's not going out much.'

'They'll be feeling their age,' said Mrs Rider. 'I know how it is. I lost my mother in the spring. Eighty-four she was—wonderful for her age.'

Believe it or not, the fronts of late-Victorian gothic houses have no fewer than twenty-one windows, counting each panel of the attic ones as a single window. To number them correctly takes at least a quarter of a minute, demanding considerable concentration and quite banishing other thoughts from the mind.

'You're looking peaky, dear,' said Mrs Rider. 'Tired. Working you hard at school, are they?'

'Sorry?'

'I thought you weren't with me. There, you get along into the warm. You must be perished, with those bare legs.'

'Yes,' said Clare, 'they are cold. Goodnight.'

She put the bike away and went in at the back door. There wasn't much warm to get on into—inside felt much the same as out, though not quite so draughty.

Tea took longer than usual. The aunts were feeling spry and talkative. They sat on either side of the library fire, swathed in plaid travelling rugs used for family holidays in the Highlands half a century and a world war ago, and wanted to be told about things outside, beyond the library and the house and Norham Gardens. They wanted to know what Clare was doing in history now, and what the new French teacher was like, and how the school production of *Macbeth* was getting along.

'I took the spears. Mrs Cramp thought they were lovely, but she was a bit fussed about the points.'

'An interesting play,' said Aunt Susan. 'What are you doing about the ghosts?'

'Doing about them?'

'Well, are you presenting them in the flesh, or keeping them as a manifestation of Macbeth's state of mind?'

'We're having them real. Banquo, anyway. He's Liz wrapped up in white cheesecloth with splashes of red paint for blood.'

'That sounds most effective,' said Aunt Anne. Wisps of hair had escaped from her knot, as they always did when she became excited in conversation, and fluttered around her face in the draught from the chimney.

Aunt Susan didn't agree. 'They are psychological ghosts. You shouldn't see them. They are an indication of Macbeth's private guilt and anguish.'

'Surely you are being too modern?' said Aunt Anne, retrieving hair. 'To the seventeenth-century mind ghosts were perfectly acceptable. Portents, maybe, expressions of guilt, if you like, but quite real and visible.'

The aunts argued, gently. The library clock whirred, clicked, struck five.

'What do people have now, then?' said Clare. 'Instead of ghosts?'

'Have?'

'Have in their minds, instead of ghosts. If they're in a state about something, like Macbeth?'

'I suppose obsessions would be the modern substitute,' said Aunt Susan. 'Neuroses of one kind and another. Burying anxiety in some kind of obsessive fancy.'

'Imagining something was going on that wasn't?'

'That kind of thing.'

'Do you remember,' said Aunt Anne, 'that poor friend of father's who thought people were in the habit of coming into his rooms at night to steal his papers? He built barricades to keep them out. It was all to do with some problem over his work. A mathematician, he was.'

'Surely he was a theologian. A man called Robinson.'

'No, no. You are confusing him with the chaplain.'

The aunts had retreated, as they sometimes did, to some time around 1930. To bring them back, Clare said, 'What happened in the end?'

'He recovered, if I remember rightly.'

'I s'pose he solved the problem. But what if you had one that couldn't be solved? That was so enormous it didn't have an answer.'

'Then,' said Aunt Susan, 'it would be part of the process of living. One's life tends to be littered with insoluble problems of one kind or another.'

'The lady who came to school to talk to us about Growing Up said everything is a matter of coming to terms and adjusting yourself. She was talking about sex, mostly.'

'If I may say so,' said Aunt Susan, 'she was entirely wrong. People are seldom adjustable. They endure. Or not, as the case may be.'

'I see,' said Clare. She got up. 'I'll have to go now. I've got homework.'

The aunts, by the fire, bargained with one another for pieces of the newspaper. The crossword puzzle was traded for the leading article. Clare closed the door and went upstairs to her room.

There was no paper in the drawer of her desk. She crossed the landing to the big drawing-room and went to get some from the desk by the window. It was bitterly cold in there, but she stood for a minute looking round at the stiff chairs and sofas standing against the wall or drawn up face to face as though locked in argument. This room had been little used for a long time now. It had been furnished and decorated for great-grandmother, who had given tea-parties here, and been At Home to her friends, and since then it had decayed quietly and privately. The curtains were faded in stripes, and the William Morris wallpaper had brown marks on it, and damp patches. The silk cushions had holes in them. The aunts' lives had not been spent in a drawing-room. They were people who lived in libraries or studies. All the same, it was full of their presence. They were here, like ghosts of themselves, pre-served at various points in their lives. On the piano, with great-grandmother, in a silver-framed photograph, Aunt Anne a plump baby in white muslin, Aunt Susan a small girl leaning against her mother's knee, staring solemn at the camera. On the mantel-piece they stood together in the preserved sunshine of some long-distant summer, young and pretty, hair piled on their heads like a cottage loaf, skirts brushing the grass. And there they were again on the desk, in separate frames, looking appropriately resolute in academic caps and gowns. And here again, on the piano, older, at a half-way point, perhaps, between the children in the picture alongside and the two people sitting at this moment in the chairs on either side of the library fire downstairs: half-way, the shape of their faces a little different, some lines now around the eyes, standing in a row of people, dark-suited men and other ladies in sober, unsmart dresses. Beneath was a small silver inscription that said 'Members of the Hope-Robertson Commission, 1939'.

Clare rummaged in the bureau for paper. Here, too, the past sur-vived time and change, petrified in letters, notes, diaries. The aunts, travelling in Italy in 1921, had written weekly to their parents, and here were the letters, bundled up and tied with white tape. Here was great-grandmother's recipe book—favourite meals recalled in a firm, sloping script. Here were letters from grandfather, killed as a young man in the First World War, and here were school reports

21

on the small son who had never known him, who was Clare's own father. She had read all these, many times, and merely tidied them into a pile before closing the drawer. No paper in there.

Other drawers yielded more letters and notebooks and, in one instance, a fat brown envelope that burst and spilled out ancient photographs of unfamiliar landscapes and dark people with painted faces and elaborate head-dresses. Clare stowed them away again and found, at last, a nice fat wad of unused sheets of paper. She took them out and went back to her room.

The next day was Saturday. Clare, waking late, came down to find Aunt Susan alone in the kitchen, putting things on a tray.

'I am defeated,' she said, 'by an apparent dearth of marmalade.'

'I expect we've run out. Where's Aunt Anne?'

'Her chest has been playing her up in the night. She thought she would stay in bed today. Dear me, I haven't put the kettle on. Somehow a methodical approach has always escaped me when it comes to domestic things. I put it down to a pampered youth.'

Clare filled the kettle. 'I'll take the tray up. Look, it's been snowing again.' The garden seemed diminished by the snow, a red brick box packed with white, lined up in a row of red brick boxes. 'I don't like snow.'

'Why ever not? It is usually exhilarating to the young. I remember *praying* for snow, quite literally, and then being consumed with guilt for bothering the Almighty over inessentials.'

'Did it work,' said Clare, 'praying?'

'Did it snow, do you mean? Presumably, in the fullness of time.'

'So you'd never have known if it was God or just the climate?'

'Exactly so. That always struck me as one of the ambiguities of prayer. We experienced religious doubts very early, Anne and I. I remember that we tried to test the matter scientifically when we were around nine or so.'

'How?'

'Oh, in small ways. We were much too scared to try tampering with anything really important. Meals, I remember—we would request a certain course of menus and wait anxiously to see what percentage of our demand was met. Above a certain proportion we felt must imply some kind of divine interference.'

'Chocolate pudding every day.'

'That kind of thing. Where do we keep butter knives?'

'In the drawer,' said Clare. 'But great-grandfather wasn't very religious, was he?'

'Dear me, no. He was interested in religion, of course, as an anthropologist. But mother was a firm believer in the proprieties, and a regular attendance at church was proper in those days, for one and all. There, I think that is all Anne will need.'

After breakfast Clare cycled into the town—along by the Parks, bleak today, dotted with prancing dogs and children skidding on the icy grass, past the University Museum and Keble with a cold hard wind gusting at her back, and then round into Broad Street and the Saturday shoppers swarming the pavements in the Cornmarket. Women with children in push-chairs, and bikes, and shiny new cars, and pop music oozing from the open doors of the new boutique, and alongside all that the black tower of St Michael's which is one thousand years old. Places are very odd, when you stop to think about it—the way they manage to be both now, and then, both at once. Much the same, if you think about it, as people.

In Boots she met Liz, from school.

'What are you doing, Clare? You've been staring at that tin of talc for about five minutes.'

'Thinking.'

'About talc?'

'No, people. Come to the library with me.'

In the Public Library Clare interpreted to a bewildered librarian the aunts' long, illegible list of books they thought they would like to read. Liz, too, needed books. She wandered disconsolately along the shelves, complaining.

'How can I know which one I want to read?'

'You couldn't ever know that till you've read it. Shut your eyes and take the seventh book from the left.'

'*Woodwork for Beginners*. Great. Just what I wanted.'

And outside it was snowing again, the dun-coloured sky whirling over the Town Hall and the traffic and the towers and spires.

'Hurray!' said Liz.

Clare said again, 'I hate snow.'

'Why on earth? It's super.'

'It makes me feel shut in. I get all anxious.'

'Don't be daft. Come to Port Meadow this afternoon.'

'I might.'

There was ice on Port Meadow, where the river had flooded over into the fields and then frozen. It was too thin to skate on, and choppy with hummocks of grass, but there were gulls careering high above in a vast pale sky and boats on the hidden river that seemed mysteriously to glide through the grass. Pakistani boys played cricket on a spread of concrete, the ball cracking down into icy puddles, shouting to each other with Oxfordshire accents. Clare cycled with Liz and others, riding fast with scarves flying, through the small back streets beyond Walton Street. She came home on fire, her face aching against the cold, her throat sore from shrieking and laughing, and wanted suddenly to give the aunts a present because they had not been there too, but the shops were shut and anyway she had no money.

Back at Norham Gardens, making tea, she remembered the Christmas roses. At the far end of the garden, under the wall, there was a place where Christmas roses grew, left over from years ago when the garden had been cherished and cared for. They must be very persistent, Christmas roses. She put on wellingtons and went out into the dusk to find them. There they were, flowering under a coating of snow, pale green ones and mauve. She picked them all, the stems dripping down her sleeve.

It was a very grey dusk, quite colourless, like a photograph—white snow and grey houses and blue-grey sky and black trees. Here and there an uncurtained window made an orange square within the dark and solid outline of the houses. Next door, someone came for a moment and stood within one of the orange squares, looking out, a stark head-and-shoulder shape, like the shape of the piece of wood from the trunk in the attic. Clare thought of it, staring from where she had put it in her own attic, over the roofs and trees. You wouldn't be able to see that, though, from outside. Just the black of the window pane. The windows of the house all glittered blackly, or sometimes white when they reflected the snow.

Clare, going back across the lawn, could see herself in the kitchen window, a black figure advancing out of a blank white square.

Except that the square wasn't quite blank. Somewhere at the back of it, behind her, there were these spiny things sticking straight up, massed together, quivering slightly, like a forest of spears, or bows and arrows, and behind them, hidden among them, shapes, forms?

She looked back. Branches, of course, branches of trees, twigs, trunks. They'd gone from the reflection now, anyway, and there was only her, holding the Christmas roses, and the telephone wires singing in the wind, like voices, far away, shouting. She shook the water off the Christmas roses and went into the house. The aunts would be pleased. They would have forgotten all about the Christmas roses. She would arrange them in one of the Lalique vases and put them on the tea-tray, for a surprise.

Aunt Anne was feeling a bit better. She had come down.

'Christmas roses! Susan, she has brought Christmas roses from the garden!'

'An inspiration! Clever child.'

The roses, pale and unreal, like imaginary flowers, flopped over the edge of the vase and made blurred reflections of themselves on the surface of the library table.

'They must have been planted before the war.'

'During Munich. I remember perfectly. One kept coming in from the garden to listen to the news.'

When you are old you remember things quite well if they happened years and years ago: it is yesterday that becomes unclear, or last week. The aunts drank tea, and looked at the Christmas roses. Clocks ticked, the fire sighed and shifted. If there was a world beyond Norham Gardens, where urgent and consuming things went on, it seemed very far away. Clare thought: I am like the aunts, we are both at a time when nothing much is happening to us. They have finished having things happen to them, and I haven't started yet. We just wait. The aunts think backwards mostly, because that suits them best. Perhaps I should think forwards, but I can't because there is nothing to be seen for certain except O levels and August in Norfolk. I don't know what I will be, any more than I am sure what I am now. I am like a chrysalis, turning into something: not knowing what is frightening, sometimes.

'More tea, dear?'

I might be someone awful. A Hitler. So that it would be better to stop now. Or I might be someone very wise and good. A great poet. Probably neither, in the end, but somewhere in between, like most people.

'Yes, please.'

Waiting to find out what will happen is like being one of the stuffed birds in the thing on the mantelpiece, sitting inside a glass dome in the middle of a Sunday afternoon that is going on for ever and ever, having peculiar thoughts that you couldn't possibly tell anyone.

'Clare! You're in a dream, child!'

'A penny for them?' said Aunt Susan.

Clare poked the fire, and created chaos, in miniature: volcanoes were born, and died, landscapes disintegrated.

'Decimal or old?'

'A penny.'

Decimal coinage the aunts ignored. They were too old, they said, to be expected to come to terms with it. Like royalty, they no longer handled money: all necessary transactions were dealt with by Mrs Hedges or Clare.

'I've forgotten now, anyway.'

Clare read, the words moving in front of her eyes, their meaning pushed aside by thoughts. It was good this afternoon, on Port Meadow. Now I feel shut in again, somehow. As though everything had stood still and I couldn't make it move. I wish it wasn't winter. Now seems to go on for ever and ever, but it isn't, you know that really—it's rushing, in fact, rushing and rushing and you can't do anything about that either.

She stared at the aunts, tranquil in the firelight, and tried again to read. Presently the thoughts lost their insistence and the words won: a strange and distant world moved into the library at Norham Gardens, a world of forests and birds of paradise and inscrutable beliefs.

CHAPTER 3

The people live and die in the valley. They are locked away from the world by mountains: by the green moss-forests and the high blue peaks. Time has stopped here. Isolated, they have known no influences, learned no skills. They know only the cycle of a man's life: birth, and maturity, and death. Their lives are both simple and deeply mysterious: they have never learned to bake clay, but they have sought explanations for their own existence. They celebrate the mystery of life with ritual. The tamburan is a part of this ritual: it is no longer an object, but a symbol.

Sunday. The snow had melted around the house, but it lay cleanly in the garden, drifted against walls and shrubs. Mrs Rider's cat picked its way across it, distasteful, leaving a trail of blue prints. The streets were quiet, the houses withdrawn, seemingly empty, in their packing of dark trees. Only the Parks exploded with sound: children squealing, dogs, snowballs, people running.

Maureen came downstairs in a candlewick dressing-gown and said her gas-ring was playing up. 'All right if I do myself an egg down here?'

'Fine,' said Clare.

'Fancy some bacon while I'm about it?'

'Yes, please.'

They ate, each side of the kitchen table. Maureen was good at bacon and eggs. Aunt Susan pottered in, looking for her glasses, and had a conversation with Maureen about how cold it was and about a winter Aunt Susan remembered when there had been skating on Port Meadow for three weeks on end. Maureen's relationship with the aunts was gingerly: she treated them with a combination of respect, amusement, and bewilderment. 'I never came across anyone quite like them before,' she confided to Clare. 'You don't know how to take them, quite. But they're a couple of old dears, really, I'd say.' The aunts, on the other hand, had perhaps not come across too many people like Maureen, but that affected them not at all: they always remained themselves under all circumstances. Aunt Susan went away again, having found her glasses in the larder. Aunt Anne had stayed in bed again.

'Is she poorly?' said Maureen.

'Not specially. She gets colds in winter.'

'My gran did that. Shocking. Ever so fond of her we were.'

Maureen smoked. Clare read.

'Novel, is it?'

'No. It's a book about New Guinea.'

'Where's that when it's at home? No, don't tell me—it's near Australia.'

'Mmn.'

'I'm not that keen on travel books, personally.'

'It's about the people, really, more than the place. They're still living in the Stone Age, you see. They were only discovered—oh, at the end of the nineteenth century, I think. Lots of different tribes. Hundreds of thousands of people—they're still discovering new lots.'

'Fancy.'

'They don't know about time, or history, or anything. They just kind of go on, living and dying, over and over again, without knowing anything about themselves. But they think their ancestors are terribly important. They worship them, really.'

'I like a nice romance,' said Maureen, 'personally.'

'My great-grandfather went there. He went on something called the Cooke Daniels expedition, in 1905. He was one of the first Europeans to visit some of the tribes.'

'Now, historical I quite like. So long as it's got love in it.'

'He brought all these things back for the Pitt Rivers museum here. Things these people made and wore,' said Clare.

'Explorer, was he? That sort of thing I quite like—jungles and crocodiles—good and steamy.'

'Anthropologist.'

'That's right,' said Maureen, yawning. 'You ought to try Jean Plaidy. She does a lovely romance. And the Nurse Duncan books. I like a nice hospital story.'

Liz came for tea in the afternoon. People liked coming to tea at Norham Gardens. They found the house extraordinary and entertaining, the aunts lovable, and they envied Clare for being allowed to do what she liked in the kitchen. They had mothers who resisted cookery experiments. Clare, of course, had Mrs Hedges, who had been known to react strongly, but her anger had to be confined to notes left on the kitchen table, which carried less force. Clare and Liz had baked beans and hot chocolate in the kitchen. Then they did their homework, one on each side of the table, cosy, with the wireless chattering to itself in the background.

'I've never seen a radio like that before,' said Liz. 'It's like in old films about the war.'

'You wouldn't. There aren't any others. The British Museum are always on at us, asking for it.'

'Idiot. Can I wind the lift up?'

Visitors were always fascinated by the lift. It sat in the corner of the kitchen, a mobile cupboard that, when you wound the handle at its side, lumbered up through the house, vanishing through a trap door in the kitchen ceiling and continuing on a rumbling progress through the house until it reached the top floor. It was a legacy of the days of cooks and parlourmaids and chambermaids.

The lift creaked up, laboriously, and down. 'Great!' said Liz.

'Step back into the past,' said Clare. 'In this house we preserve an older, finer way of life. Welcome to nineteen thirty-six.'

'What were the bells for?'

'If you were in the drawing-room and you wanted someone to bring you more coal for the fire you rang the bell and one of those round things flipped over and someone down here saw and rushed up to see what was wrong.'

'Gosh. You are *lucky*. Living in a weird house like this. Ours is the same as the one next door and the one opposite and about half a million others.'

'So's this,' said Clare. 'The same as the one next door.'

'At least they're both weird.'

'Ssh. I've got yards and yards of Latin to do. What's the future of moriar?'

'What?'

'They will die.'

'Moriarunt. It's passive. Daft—typical stupid Latin. It's something you do, not something you have done to you.'

Clare said, 'Is it?'

'Yes, of course. Which sentence are you on? Wake up!'

'Sorry. The general. Fearing the arrival of reinforcements from Gaul. Have you got my dictionary?'

'No.'

'I must have left it upstairs. Come up with me.'

Clare's room was on the second floor, opposite the aunt's room, between two empty ones.

'How on earth,' said Liz, 'do you decide which rooms to live in? With so many.'

'We move around with the seasons. Follow the sun. Face south in winter.'

'You don't.'

'Joke. The aunts have always had the back ones and I like this one because it looks out over the Parks.'

'It's even untidier than mine,' said Liz. 'And that's saying something.'

'Mrs Hedges calls it The Slump. She says it sends her into a depression just thinking about coming in here. So she mostly doesn't.'

'Lucky you.'

The dictionary was under a pile of jerseys and underclothes.

'Look at the Parks,' said Liz. 'The snow ...'

The Parks were a wilderness, not tamed any more with cricket and football pitches, but bleak and pathless. The trees stood out, evergreens crouching black and the stripped winter outlines of beech and chestnut rattling and shifting in the wind. There was hardly anyone about—just here and there a hurrying pin-figure. The laboratories on the far side must have people in them, looking through microscopes, reading, writing, but they looked abandoned, left empty in the aftermath of some terrible disaster.

'You can't remember what it's like in summer,' said Clare.

'No. Willows, and long grass.'

'Punts.'

'People playing cricket. Ice cream.'

'You feel as though it was stuck at now, for ever and ever.' Clare stared out; there was so little moving, out there, that it could have been a painting or a stage-set. A background to some enacted drama.

'I read a short story about that once. The world gets stuck at winter, somehow, and it never gets any warmer and nothing grows and everyone dies.'

'I don't feel as though the world was stuck. Just me.'

'Can I see the hats?' said Liz.

Clare's visitors always wanted to see the hats, along with the lift and the china collection in the drawing-room and the old photograph albums in the study desk. 'It's super coming here,' they said happily. 'Like a museum where you're allowed to take everything out and mess about with it.'

'All right,' said Clare. 'Come on.'

Clare's great-grandmother, unlike her daughters, Aunt Anne and Aunt Susan, had been a lady of fashion. While her husband roamed the world in search of primitive peoples, and, back in Oxford, shut himself away with his books to puzzle out the relevance of their mysterious lives, great-grandmother attended garden parties and theatres and entertained her friends to luncheon and afternoon tea and dinner in the evening. The equipment that had been necessary for all these activities, the dresses and capes and gloves and boots, and, above all, the battery of elaborate hats, feathered, ribboned, and flowered, lay still in trunks in the attic. The aunts had never needed such things, but it did not occur to them to get rid of them, and in any case when Aunt Anne and Aunt Susan had needed something more ornate than the baggy tweed suits they had worn all their lives, they raided the trunks, and sallied forth to a wedding or a lunch inappropriately but, they felt, correctly dressed.

They had to move some bundles of old curtains and a heap of cushions to get at the hat trunk. Mrs Hedges must have been tidying again.

Liz rummaged, enthralled. 'Oh! I've never seen this one before, with the long velvet ribbons. Gorgeous ...' They propped a long mirror up against the wall and examined themselves.

'You need piled-up hair for this kind. Ours is all wrong.'

'Hang on—there are some comb things up here.'

'That's better. Gosh ... I wish I wasn't so spotty. I bet your great-grandmother wasn't spotty.'

'That one has a dress to go with it. Wait a minute.'

The dress was pale lilac, encrusted with lace, cunningly engineered over substructures of canvas and whalebone. Liz struggled into it.

'It's no good. I can't fill it out at the top and it won't go round me in the middle.'

'You're the wrong shape. They squeezed themselves in at the waist, then, so that they bulged out either side.'

'I wish I looked like that. All majestic.' Liz peered disconsolately downwards, at the coffee lace bosom of the dress caving in on her white cotton vest and bony chest.

'You never know. You might later on.'

'Some hope. Can I have that feather thing? How does it go? Just round and round you?'

Clare opened another trunk. Somewhere, she knew, there was an evening dress all decorated with sequins, and an ostrich feather affair for the head, that matched it. Liz would like that. Funny, really, great-grandmother accumulating all this stuff and great-grandfather going all the way to Australia to get things not so very different for the Pitt Rivers museum. Great-grandmother, though, from what one heard of her, wouldn't fancy the comparison with primitive tribesmen.

Liz shrieked.

'What on earth's the matter?'

'What's that ghastly thing?'

'This? I'm not sure, really. Maureen and I found it the other day.'

'I saw it looking at me in the mirror. Like a face.'

It had slipped slightly: someone must have knocked against it. Clare put it straight again. It did not look quite as dingy as she remembered. The reds and blacks of the outlining seemed a little sharper, perhaps because she had switched an extra light on.

'Why on earth do you have it there? It gives me the shivers.'

'I don't know,' said Clare. 'I just felt I should. I don't know why, at all.'

'Help me get this off—I don't want to tear the lace.'

The door opened.

'Excuse me,' said Maureen, 'I thought someone had forgotten the light.'

Clare said, 'This is Liz.'

'Hello,' said Liz.

'Hello. What's this, then? Fancy dress parade?'

'They're my great-grandmother's things.'

Maureen fingered the material. 'Must have cost a bomb, that. You don't get cloth like that, nowadays. And those hats. You should try some of this stuff on a museum, or theatrical people— you'd get quite a bit for it, I should think.'

'No,' said Clare, 'that wouldn't be a very good idea.'

'Help!' said Liz, floundering in lilac silk.

'Your friend seems to be having a spot of bother,' said Maureen. 'Well, I'd better make tracks. I'm going to the pictures. With a girl from the office, in case you're thinking otherwise. Bye for now.'

They put the dresses away and went downstairs to finish their homework. Aunt Susan came into the kitchen and helped with the Latin translation. For people who could not (or would not) cope with decimals, the aunts were amazingly competent when it came to Latin. Aunt Susan unravelled six sentences of the most perverse construction, and glowed a little with self-satisfaction.

'One is not entirely useless yet.'

She could also, it turned out, help explain the complexities of Elizabeth I's foreign policy. Then she went away to do *The Times* crossword in the library.

'I love your aunts,' said Liz.

'They're all right.'

Liz was fetched by her father, in a car, and went away into the night. Maureen came down in a red coat with a fur collar, to meet her friend and spend the evening watching stylised violence at the Super. Clare and Aunt Susan sat by the fire, sharing a rug across their knees. It was very cold. Upstairs, Aunt Anne slept in the big front bedroom which had been hers for the last forty years. Outside, the temperature fell. Frost clutched the trees and bushes, and the slush on the roads hardened into ice. The cars in Norham Gardens passed with a hard, cracking sound.

There was a fresh fall of snow. It distorted the familiar landscape of houses and streets in a way that Clare found unsettling. She felt trapped by the leaden sky and the cold. The houses, picked out with snow along ledges and gables, seemed different—diminished, less secure. The trees, the chestnuts and flowering cherries and copper beeches of suburban streets, had become wilder: they hinted at Siberian forests and vast primeval woodlands. They no longer existed by courtesy, restrained by fence and wall and pavement, but dominated the place, as though they might expand and grow, splitting concrete, toppling brick. Looking out of the kitchen window, she saw Mrs Rider's cat transformed into a panther, crouched on the garden wall, waiting for the birds that hopped despondent in the snow. The wireless talked with gloomy satisfaction of freeze-ups and traffic chaos: somewhere out there, in the rest of England, lorry drivers were marooned on Shap Fell and angry commuters waited in trainless stations.

Maureen said it was silly to ride that bike to school, you could come a cropper on the ice, and Clare, not disposed to argue, went to and fro on the bus, huddled companionably against people buried deep in winter coats, trailing scarves and shopping baskets and school satchels. The conductor was West Indian, but when he spoke it was with the voice of Midland England, underpinned somewhere far beneath with an alien rhythm, a memory of sun and sea and bananas. He was possessed with cheerfulness, joking, smiling, nipping back and forth and up and down the stairs with the agility of a sailor riding unsteady seas. Doesn't he mind the snow? Clare wondered, the cold? or has he been here so long he doesn't remember being hot in the winter? And sitting there, squashed up against a woman, so close you could feel the warmth of her, hear her breathe, she thought, how odd you can be so close to someone and not know anything about them, nothing at all. She might be a murderer, or famous, and I wouldn't know. I only know about the conductor because I can see he's West Indian, and hear it. That's why people have to talk to each other, all the time. If you couldn't talk to people, tell them about yourself, you'd go mad.

School was all talk, of course, but in a different way. Being told, not telling. Mostly, it was a part of the long Sunday afternoon. You were listening, but a part of you was just sleeping through it, waiting. Not entirely, of course, because it was not without drama: you could, within the compass of a single day, go the whole way from despair to exaltation. But it was like the landscapes in the fireplace at Norham Gardens: worlds could disintegrate, but tomorrow, or next week, everything would be the same again.

You sat at your desk by the window, and heard about anguish and guilt, passion and grief, Macbeth, Heathcliff, Cathy. And beyond the door the dinner bell rang and people clattered down the stairs to play hockey in North Oxford. Wars were chalked up on the blackboard, and the death of kings, and disposed of in a shower of chalk dust, whole populations wiped out to make way for the declension of a Latin verb. Somewhere, there was a place where these things happened, a place of decision and disaster, but it could be contained between the pages of books and tidied away to make room for the real world of piano lessons and dinner tickets and home at ten to four.

The products of Australia, says Miss Hammond, are meat, and fruit, and grain. The climate is arid, the deserts waterless. Sydney exports tinned peaches. The aborigines eat frogs and lizards, believe that men can be killed by means of magic. 'In New Guinea,' says Clare, 'people think their ancestors are spirits. They talk to them, just like they talk to each other.'

Miss Hammond smiles. She likes people to show an interest.

Yes, she says, the customs of primitive tribes are interesting. How did you know that, she says? 'I read a book.' And there's this thing in my attic, I don't quite know what it is, what it means, something my great-grandfather brought here. Liz and Maureen think it's creepy. I don't really. Beautiful, in a funny way. Sad, somehow, but I don't know why.

Outside, the white skies press down on the city. It snows.

There was a note from Mrs Hedges on the kitchen table: 'Your Aunt Anne doesn't look too good to me. I wanted to have the doctor in but she wasn't having it. Do they understand you don't pay any more? Be a good girl and see she stays in the warm this evening.'

Clare took tea up to Aunt Anne, in bed. The gas-fire was burning low, a sulky blue: she turned it up. Aunt Anne looked small in the middle of the large bed, swathed in very old cardigans.

'How are you feeling?'

'Perfectly all right. Just a stupid cough. Susan is fussing.'

Clare said severely, 'You should have let Mrs Hedges get the doctor.'

'Quite unnecessary.'

'Tomorrow, then.'

'We'll see. I'll come down later.'

'No.'

'I am being bullied,' said Aunt Anne. She sounded tired.

Clare wandered around the room, touching the brushes on the dressing-table, picking up a photograph, drawing the curtains. There was nothing in the room less than twenty years old: only the view out of the window admitted intrusions where cranes and scaffolding broke the skyline of house, tree and lamp-post. A few streets away, a new college was being built. Bulldozers and cement-mixers rumbled in the muddy landscape that had once been houses and gardens. Cycling past, a day or so before, she had noticed the solitary old tree allowed to survive beside the new building outlined in girders and concrete.

Aunt Anne said, 'What have you done today?'

'Nothing.'

'Nothing! An entire day with nothing done at all!'

'Well, I've done things—geography and maths and eating meals and coming home—but without really knowing about it, if you see what I mean.'

'Perfectly,' said Aunt Anne.

'Quite a lot of days are like that.'

'It's one of the trials of being young, I'm afraid.'

'You're supposed to be having a good time every minute,' said Clare. 'Like people in advertisements—you know, floating through fields eating chocolate, or rushing about drinking coke on enormous beaches.' She examined the photograph by the bed: sometime long ago a person in a skirt to her ankles—Aunt Susan?—threw a stick for a dog, beside the sea. 'Actually it's not like that at all. At least I don't think it is.'

'Of course it isn't,' said Aunt Anne. 'Only very unperceptive people could suppose otherwise.'

'Mostly you're just waiting for something to happen. Or wondering what it'll be like when it does.'

'Exactly.'

'Would you like to be fourteen?'

'Not in the least,' said Aunt Anne cheerfully. 'I wonder if you could very kindly give me that unpleasant medicine by the wash-basin?'

'Perhaps I'm specially bad at it?'

'Bad at what?'

'Being fourteen.'

'I shouldn't think so. There is a rather regrettable tendency nowadays to fence people off according to age. The "young"—as though they were some particular breed. A misleading idea, on the whole. Perhaps you are just not good at being fenced off.'

'Oh. I see.'

'The same is done to us, of course. The old. This medicine is quite remarkably nasty.'

'Have a cup of tea, quick. Do you feel fenced off?'

'Only by the tiresome business of one's joints going stiff, and one's teeth falling out, and not hearing so well. Otherwise one is much the same person as one has always been, and the world is no less interesting a place, I promise you.' Aunt Anne heaved herself further up on the pillows, and drank tea. Her bun, never entirely secure, had come loose and long strands of brown hair streaked with grey lay around her shoulders. She coughed. 'Would you remind Susan, when you go down, that according to my reckoning it is about my turn for the newspaper?'

Going downstairs, Clare thought, talking to the aunts is as easy as talking to people at school, in a different way. Liz, or someone. That's what Aunt Anne means by not being fenced off. They're terribly old, the aunts, but somehow I never think about that, except when other people go on about it. Funny, when you think how different the insides of their heads must be, so much fuller than mine, not just knowing more things, like which Prime Minister came after Lloyd George, but all the things they've seen and done and said. All that stays in people's heads, it must do, that's the difference between being old and young, in the end.

Lying in bed that night, in the hinterland between being awake and asleep, when things slide agreeably from what is real to what is not, it seemed to her that the house itself, silent around her, was a huge head, packed with events and experiences and conversations. And she was part of them, something the house was storing up, like people store each other up. Drifting into sleep, she imagined words lying around the place like bricks, all the things people had said to each other here, piled up in the rooms like the columns of books and papers in the library, and she wandered around among them, pushing through them, jostled by them.

And later still, she returned to the place where the brown people had been. She found herself back there with a feeling that there was something she had left uncompleted, and hurried down the path towards the clearing with a determination that this time she must speak to them. They could not, after all, harm her in any way. It was a dream, and nothing in a dream is real.

Knowing this, she was interested to find that at the same time she could feel the heat of the sun on her arm, and smell the strong, slightly rotten smell that came from some orchid-like flowers that trailed from a branch. She thought, with amusement, that she must be one of the few people to have walked through a jungle in their nightdress. Something rustling in the undergrowth made her stop for a moment, and when it exploded on to the path in the form of one of the pig-like animals, she jumped. It stared at her for a moment, bristling, with little red eyes, and she was glad when it turned and trotted away into the bamboo again.

Coming suddenly into the clearing she was surprised to find it empty, the fires dead and the people nowhere to be seen. All the same, she felt certain that they were near. She went up to one of the huts and peered inside. Eyes met hers from the darkness, and as she became used to the gloom she could see them sitting there, watching her. She saw too that their faces were most elaborately painted, in reds, blacks and yellows, which she had not noticed before, though now it seemed the most important thing about them, and that their expressions beneath the paint were both frightened and sad.

And then a very curious thing happened. She spoke to them, and they replied, but no language passed between them. No language passed, but she was perfectly clear that they were asking her for something. They were saying that she had something to give them, and they needed it. This embarrassed and disturbed her, and the embarrassment turned to fear as they got up, one by one, and began to move towards her. But as her fear swelled to panic she realised that to escape the situation she had only to wake up, and did so, though a little less easily than before, with the feeling that she was extracting herself with difficulty from something, dragging herself upwards rather than simply floating free. In the morning she remembered nothing at all, except again, that she had dreamed, and that the dream produced a nagging sense of some obligation unfulfilled.

CHAPTER 4

The man who made the tamburan sits before his fire in the dawn. Pigs and children move around him. In the trees birds of paradise are calling, and cockatoos. The sun is not yet up and mist lies along the floor of the valley. He eats yam, and stares into the fire. He lives in a world of total insecurity: he may die in the next five minutes, or tomorrow, or before the next moon. He has no protection against the spears of his enemies, except his own spear and arrows, nor any against the sorcery that is a daily threat, except the protection of the ancestors. The man, knowing that sorcery has caused his yam plants to wither, consults the tamburan: accepting death, and yet denying it, he is not separated from his grandfather or his great-grandfather. They live on, protective and influential, represented by objects.

'There's this fight,' said Maureen, 'in the caff. Only you don't see all of it, not the blood and that. You see them get their knives out, and their faces—the expressions. And there's loud music. You don't see what they do, exactly. You're kind of left to guess.'

'I see,' said Clare.

'It's not a good film if you're the imaginative type. It was all right in a way, but I don't know if I'd want to see it round again.'

'I've been to *Romeo and Juliet* at the Playhouse. You see all the sword fight in that. I suppose there could be blood, if they made a mistake.'

'They'd be trained,' said Maureen. 'You couldn't have a mess, not with all the audience sitting there.'

'It was super.'

Maureen said, 'He's good, Shakespeare.' She began to collect the plates and run water in the sink. They had taken to breakfasting together in the kitchen every day now. The milkman came round the side of the house, clinking bottles, and Maureen watched through the side of the curtain, still running water into the sink and putting plates under the tap. She was interested in the milkman. She could fancy him, she said. The male world was divided, as far as Maureen was concerned, into those you couldn't fancy at any price, and those you could, given certain circumstances that were never quite specified. Maureen never went so far as to do any positive fancying.

The milkman went away and Maureen said, 'There were these two fellows came up to us after—me and my friend, that is. They said would we like a drink. They'd got a nerve, I'll say that.'

'Did you fancy them?' said Clare with interest.

Maureen snorted. 'No, thank you very much. I'm not the type that lets herself get picked up.'

'Suppose the milkman said would you like a drink? Other than milk, I mean.'

'I'd be making myself cheap.'

'Oh,' said Clare, disappointed. A romance between Maureen and the milkman would have been fun. One could have stood around at the edges, as it were, feeling involved at one remove.

'My friend's good-looking,' said Maureen. 'Twenty-three, she is.' The plates were being slapped down on the draining-board now, a bit too sharply. 'She's got a boy friend. But he's in Leeds this week. That's why she came to the pictures.'

'Oh, I see.'

'They'll be getting married at Easter. A white wedding, she's going to have.' One of the plates, slapped too hard, cracked in half. 'I'm sorry about that. I'll pay for it.'

'It doesn't matter,' said Clare. 'We've got masses more.' She watched Maureen tidy her hair and put on lipstick, ready to go to work. 'I like your jersey. You look nice in blue.'

Maureen did not answer, pursing her mouth at the mirror, armouring herself against the morning. She put the lipstick in her bag, picked up her coat and said, 'They're a new line at Marks.' She inspected her reflection again. 'Oh well, hope springs eternal. See you later.'

Clare drank tea, slowly, reluctant to go outside and start the day. She flicked over the pages of a magazine Maureen had left on the table, reading here and there. Maureen's magazine offered solutions to everything: acne, period pains, split ends, depression. From every page girls smiled or frowned—despondent on Monday with greasy hair, radiant on Friday with a new boy friend, all uncertainties resolved by change of shampoo. They trooped from one bright picture to another, uniformly young and pretty, in a world where everything was clear and new. They whooped through misty landscapes in their underclothes, rose like Venus from the sea, hair streaming in the wind. On one page a girl sat sleekly on a bar stool, sipping from a tall glass, watched admiringly by spruce young men, having fun. 'One day,' the caption warned, 'you'll be too old for it': behind, a size smaller, the barman watched unsmiling, too old.

The kitchen clock whirred and clicked for a quarter to nine. Clare put the magazine on the dresser and collected her coat, scarf, satchel of books.

She could hear Aunt Susan coming downstairs, slowly, one step at a time. She'd be holding on to the banisters, looking out for the loose stair-rod. 'Broken limbs are a perfect nuisance at our age. One must just be that much more careful.'

They met in the hall.

'How's Aunt Anne?'

'I don't like this cold. We must have the doctor, Clare, and never mind the expense. I've told her to stop being silly.'

'You don't pay any more,' said Clare. 'Not for years. We explained, Mrs Hedges and me. It's all free.'

Aunt Susan said 'Yes, dear,' in the voice that meant she wasn't taking something in.

'I'll go to the surgery on the way to school. It's always engaged if you telephone.'

'We like a lady doctor,' said Aunt Susan.

'I don't think they've got one. I'll ask, though.'

The surgery was crowded. Every chair was filled. People eyed each other with suspicion, guarding the order of precedence, jumping as the doctor's bell rang. A baby wailed. Small children stared and fidgeted. A man in a donkey jacket and mud-stained boots tucked a cigarette stub into the corner of his mouth and read *Good Housekeeping*, turning the pages with huge fingers. There was a smell of people: sweat and clothes and soap and tobacco.

The receptionist said, 'Surgery's full for this morning. Are you an emergency?'

Am I? Not in any obvious way.

'I don't want to see the doctor. My aunt's ill. Miss Mayfield. Forty Norham Gardens.'

'No home calls,' said the receptionist, 'except for emergencies and the elderly without transport.' She allowed herself a faint, triumphant smile.

'She's that,' said Clare, 'the elderly without transport.' Game, set and match.

The triumphant smile went away and became a thin, resentful look. The receptionist wrote down the address, with a sigh. She had smeary glasses and a large spot on her chin that had been carefully powdered over but still showed. Perhaps, Clare thought, she was in love with the doctor and thought she must protect him from hordes of hysterical, demanding patients. Or perhaps she was just nasty.

'It'll be afternoon. His list's overloaded already.'

'All right.'

'Or evening. I couldn't say.'

Clare went. People, bundled into coats and scarves, were coming up the doctor's gravelled drive, bringing him coughs and septic fingers and sleeplessness and indeterminate pains. That receptionist would keep the numbers down, though: you'd have to be pretty fit just to get past her. The really frail patients she presumably finished off, just by looking at them.

The north wind was driving straight down Banbury Road, bleak and untamed, all the way from Yorkshire and Scotland and beyond that still. The sky was white, the trees black and spiny against it, the branches dazzling to look at, like an optical illusion. It was nine o'clock. Wednesday. The third week in January.

At four o'clock Banbury Road was precisely the same, except that the ice on the pavements had slackened once again into slush. The sky was as white, the trees as black. The cars whipped back and forth, and in the greengrocer's people told each other what a shocking winter it was, and how there'd be more before it was over. Clare bought oranges, and a steamed pudding in a tin.

Back at Norham Gardens, Mrs Hedges was in the kitchen, surprisingly, drinking tea. 'I thought I'd just stop in for the doctor, till you got back. Your Aunt Susan doesn't always hear the bell.'

'Thanks,' said Clare. 'The receptionist person didn't want to let him come, but I said she was the elderly without transport.'

Mrs Hedges poured a cup of tea. 'Here, you look perished. They think they're God Almighty, that type. You've just got to take no notice.'

'Won't your husband be wanting his tea? And Linda.'

'They'll have to wait, won't they?' said Mrs Hedges. 'Do them no harm. Maybe Linda'll have thought to light the fire, for once. You don't look well to me, you know. Washed out. Is anything wrong?'

'No.'

'Bags under your eyes. Been going to bed at all hours, I don't doubt.'

'Not really. I have these dreams.'

'What dreams?'

'Dreams, just.'

'I'm bringing you that tonic Linda had last winter,' said Mrs Hedges firmly. 'Run down, you must be.'

'Thank you,' said Clare. 'Do tonics stop you dreaming?'

Mrs Hedges put her coat on, and woolly gloves. 'That I couldn't tell you.'

'What I really need is a tonic that makes you better at Latin.'

'Miracles, you're asking for. How's your Miss Cooper getting on, by the way?'

'Maureen, you mean. She washes her hair on Fridays and her

best friend's getting married at Easter. In white.'

'Well, you're hitting it off together, that's obvious. It's the old ladies that have surprised me. You'd never think they'd take that easily to a lodger. Not living the way they've been used to.'

'They're not fenced off,' said Clare.

'They're not what? Oh, never mind—I know you, I'm not getting involved in one of your conversations where everything sounds back to front, or I'll be here all night.' Mrs Hedges rinsed out the cups under the tap and went to the door. 'Goodnight. And you get an early night, mind.'

'Goodnight. Thanks for staying.'

The front door banged. Mrs Hedges went away to Headington, her husband, and Linda who worked in Boots and would marry her boy friend of two years' standing on March the eighteenth. Clare spread homework over the kitchen table. Five minutes later the front door bell rang.

The doctor was in the hall as soon as the door opened. 'Which room?'

'Upstairs,' said Clare, confused. He set off up the stairs at a gallop and she had to take two steps at a time to keep up with him. He was on the landing, looking round impatiently, before she reached the top. 'This one?'

He went in, closing the door behind him, and Clare, going downstairs again, realised that she had hardly even seen him, would not recognise him again. Doctors are busy people. Do not waste your doctor's time. If that receptionist was having a love affair with him it must be conducted at breakneck speed. Like trains whisking past each other in a tunnel.

Aunt Susan, in the library, had heard the bell. 'Was that the doctor?'

'Yes. I took him up.'

'I think I'll have a little chat when he comes down. Will you bring him in here, Clare?'

Clare said, 'Yes,' doubtfully, and went out into the hall again. Three minutes later the doctor came down, pushing a stethoscope into his bag and rummaging for a prescription pad. He came to rest at the hall table, writing feverishly.

'Here, get this along to a chemist in the morning. Two tea-spoonsful before meals. And here are some tablets.'

Clare said, 'Is she all right?'

'What? Oh, nothing to worry about. Better stay indoors while this weather lasts.'

'She's rather old.'

'Quite,' said the doctor. 'Splendid old lady. Quite a few years to go yet.' He ripped the prescription off the pad and handed it to Clare, moving steadily towards the front door. 'All right, then?'

'Yes.'

'Good. Splendid. Your grandmother, is she?'

'Her name's Miss Mayfield,' said Clare.

'Quite,' said the doctor. He was ticking off addresses on a type-written list in his hand. 'Tell me, is Crick Road the one off to the left? I'm new to this practice.'

'Yes.'

'Splendid. Goodnight then.'

He was already half-way out of the door. You cannot suggest to someone moving at that speed that it would be nice if they came in for a little chat. Clare said, 'Goodnight,' to the back of his overcoat going down the steps, and closed the door. She went back into the library.

'I'm afraid he was in rather a hurry.'

'What a pity,' said Aunt Susan. 'It would have been nice to get to know him. What did he say?'

'He said there was nothing to worry about. And he left a prescription. I'll get it tomorrow.'

'That's a relief, then. I don't like these colds Anne gets. Did he seem a competent man?'

'You couldn't really tell,' said Clare.

'Is something bothering you, dear?'

'No.'

'Then that's all right,' said Aunt Susan. She unfolded *The Times* and began to read the leading article, holding the small print close to her face. Once she said, 'This business in Ireland is horribly distressing.' Her handbag slipped off her lap on to the hearthrug, but she did not notice. She breathed in little puffs, like someone who has run up a flight of stairs: there was just the sound of her breathing in the room, and the fire whistling, very quiet, and the clock ticking. Ticking and ticking. Clare got up and Aunt Susan said, still reading, 'We might have our supper in here, don't you think?' Her reading glasses had slipped down her nose and rested on the bony tip. In old photographs, the aunts had plump faces. Now, the plumpness had splintered into wrinkles. Their faces were hatched all over with lines, like old china, and underneath you could see the shape of the bones. If you touched their skin, it was very soft, like fur, and thin.

Clare said, 'Yes, it'll be warmer.' She went into the kitchen and wrote about the causes of the Civil War, for forty minutes precisely by the clock.

There was a note at the bottom of her English essay, a terse B, and then Mrs Cramp's neat red words marching across the page, saying, 'Not one of your best pieces of work, Clare. Some careless mistakes. See me after lunch.'

Mrs Cramp had four children in a village somewhere outside Oxford, and had strong feelings. She had been known to weep over *Romeo and Juliet* even on a wet Friday afternoon among the desks and blackboards of formroom D. She also voted Labour and became heated about South Africa and Enoch Powell and Rhodesia and could with great ease be diverted into long discussions about almost anything except clothes which she said were boring. She had untidy brown hair that forever escaped from a roll at the back, and somehow knew a great deal about everyone she taught. For this, and other things, she was liked. Clare liked her. If one had had a mother, someone like Mrs Cramp would have done.

Mrs Cramp was sitting behind the formroom desk with a pile of exercise books in front of her.

'Oh, Clare, yes—I wanted a word about your essay. I liked it, you know, but it was rather puzzling—so many careless mistakes, not like you at all, really. You usually write so carefully. This seemed to have been tossed off in a high passion. Had you enjoyed writing it?'

'In a way,' said Clare.

47

'Mmn ... Let's see, now ... Yes, here—"I stood in front of the house which loomed above me like a sort of memorial". Good word, memorial, but "sort of" is shocking English. Either it was a memorial or it wasn't.'

'It was,' said Clare.

'Then say so. And I don't like this bit much either: "The bull-dozers flung themselves upon the walls and gnawed at them and I saw them collapse in a cloud of dust and with them all the things that were mine and as I rushed forward it seemed to me that my own foundations were giving way too and I wouldn't any longer know who I was or what I had been." A disorganised sentence, that. You should have broken it up into two, perhaps. And here ... "I stood in the rubble where the house had been and found that I didn't know what time it was or anything or even my own name"—not "or anything", that's messy—and here, "I rushed hither and thither trying to find things that were familiar and would help me to remember what had gone before—pictures, letters, anything". "Hither and thither" is too literary, I felt. "Here and there" would have been better.'

'Yes, I see,' said Clare. 'Thank you.'

'But don't go away with the idea that I didn't like the essay, because I did. In many ways it was the best. Most people wrote very straightforward things about getting married or having their first baby.'

'You just said "Imagine a day in your own future and describe it, as though you are looking back".'

'Yes. Nobody else wrote about their house being knocked down, though. It did convey the idea of memory being something that people can't do without. And the house was well-described. Were you thinking of your aunts' house?'

'I'm not sure really.'

'How are your aunts, by the way? That was the other thing I wanted to talk to you about. I keep meaning to look in and see them—and have a chat about you.'

'Is something wrong with me?' said Clare.

Mrs Cramp laughed. 'Not that I know of. Just to talk about O levels and that kind of thing. Is everything going all right?'

'Yes, thank you,' said Clare.

Mrs Cramp looked down at the essay again. 'So what I really wanted to say was that you must remember that language is an instrument, Clare. An instrument to be used precisely. Nobody can say what they mean until they use words with precision. But you know that really, I think.' Suddenly she picked up a red biro and put two crosses after the B at the bottom of the essay. 'There, I was being too hard on you, I think. It was really rather good— carelessness aside. It had a sense of time in it, and of what it's like to get older, which most of the others didn't have. Is it something you've thought about lately?'

Chalk dust swirled in the light from the window. Hairpins jutted dangerously from the back of Mrs Cramp's head. Clare said, 'It's what nobody ever talks about. We have lessons on sex and the reproductive system about once a term. People go on about that till you get a bit bored with it, actually. What they don't tell you is how you keep changing all the time, but while you're doing it you don't really know. Only later.'

'Yes, I see,' said Mrs Cramp, stabbing hairpins back into her hair. Outside, people were shouting in the playing-fields, their voices very loud and high. 'The trouble is it's very difficult to explain. To put into words. I'm not sure I'd know how to, for one. It's much easier to draw diagrams of people's insides.'

A bell rang. People clattered in the passage. Mrs Cramp stacked the exercise books and said, 'Bother—you'll have to go.' As Clare moved to the door she said, 'You look tired. What time do you get to bed?'

'Quite early,' said Clare. 'We haven't got a telly.'

'I see. There isn't anything wrong, is there?'

'I don't think so.'

'You must say, you know. To me. Or someone.'

'Yes,' said Clare. 'Thank you.'

'Language,' said Clare to Liz, 'is an instrument. You have to use it precisely. Like a screwdriver or something. Not just bash around vaguely?'

'What *are* you on about?'

'But the trouble is that people don't. They say things like "quite" and "rather" and "ever so many" and "by and large" and "much of a muchness" and "quite a few". Now what do you suppose a person means when he says "quite a few"?'

Liz said, 'It would depend what he meant quite a few of. Bananas, or miles, or people living in Manchester.'

'Years.'

'Then it could mean anything.'

'Quite,' said Clare.

Mrs Hedges' note, propped against the teapot, said, 'See your Aunt Anne takes her medicine before dinner and last thing. Tonic for you by the sink. Apple pie in the larder.'

The tonic tasted of old hay. One felt much the same after it, moreover, neither healthier nor more intelligent, or in any other way altered. Never mind: Linda, after a winter of it, had been promoted to Senior Sales Assistant and got engaged to her boy friend. Clare put the cork back in and arranged the bottle carefully on the kitchen shelf. Doing so, she caught sight of her own face in the brown-framed mirror that had certainly hung there since 1920 something. What a pity mirrors couldn't remember faces they had reflected before. There should be some way of peeling back layers—finding the aunts, years ago, great-grandmother, parlour-maids, cooks ... The shadow of the lampshade, falling down one cheek, gave her a striped face, half light and half dark, and all of a sudden there came back to her something that had been lurking at the back of her mind all day, irritating her like the forgotten second line of a poem.

She'd dreamed in the night, again, she remembered now—dreamed she was standing at the top of the stairs when the doorbell had rung, and she'd gone on standing there for a moment, and the house had been absolutely still and silent around her. It had been like a shell, quite without life, and she'd realised that this was because the clocks had stopped, all of them. And then the bell had rung again and she'd gone down to answer it. She had opened the front door and there'd been a man there, one of the small brown men, and she had had the impression that there were more of them beyond him, somewhere outside. His face had been a painted mask, the eyes and forehead white, the cheeks yellow, the mouth red-circled, and stripes running down from hairline to jaw. Bold, bright stripes. He had said nothing, but had stared at her, and all of a sudden she had been afraid. She'd been afraid, and at the same time she had realised she was dreaming, and had fought the dream, in panic, struggling against something that seemed, strongly this time, to hold her back. There had been a moment of drowning, and then of surging upwards, and she had woken, remembering the dream, but forgetting it again until now.

She stood looking at her own face, not seeing it, thinking about other things. This house. That painted shield in the attic. The aunts. Then and now. Yesterday. Tomorrow. Outside, the snow thawed a little and dripped from the gutters. Mrs Rider's randy tom yowled along the garden walls.

CHAPTER 5

The brown children play in the morning sun: they quarrel, chase lizards, throw stones. One day, in a few years, they will become adult. Their childhood will end abruptly, with ritual and ceremonial, and they will be men and women. Their world is a precise one: they know what they are, there is no confusion. In the same way, nothing is hidden from them: they see birth, and death. They find a rat in the bamboo, and kill it. The ghosts of rats have caused pigs to die in the village: the children hang the body of the rat on a tree to warn the rat ghosts that the tribe knows what they are up to. They attend to the rat ghosts, and chew sugar-cane, and quarrel, and sing.

On Saturday morning the sun came out. It was as though a white lid were tipped aside, and behind it was this pale blue sky and wintry sun, shining benignly on the snow and the brick and black trees and gothic windows. 'Ever so pretty,' said Maureen, 'like Switzerland.' She hitched the belt of her candlewick dressing-gown and stared into the garden. 'I've sometimes thought I'd fancy a winter sports holiday.'

'The Lower Fifth went,' said Clare, 'and the Sixth. They all brought back photographs of the ski instructors. They looked like men in knitting patterns—square faces and very white teeth. All exactly the same.'

'I know that type,' said Maureen. 'Very matey and out for what they can get. No thank you very much.'

'There'd be the skiing too.'

Maureen shot a suspicious glance across the table. 'I daresay. All the same, I think I'll stick to my two weeks on the Costa Brava. You know where you are with Spain. There's the front door.'

'I'll go,' said Clare. The front door was still bolted with the chain up. It was Mrs Hedges who had insisted on the chain. 'It's not as though you've got a man in the house,' she'd said. 'And there's a lot of break-ins nowadays in North Oxford.'

'But we've got the spears,' said Clare, 'and the assegais in the drawing-room. I could hurl them from the upstairs windows, or over the banisters.' Mrs Hedges hadn't been amused. And now Maureen had discovered the chain, and endorsed Mrs Hedges' back-to-the-wall outlook. They retreated at night as though into a fortress.

Clare fought her way through the defences, and got the door open.

He was standing on the top step, looking straight in front of him, so that their eyes met as soon as the door was opened. They were brown eyes, expressionless. And the stripes ran down his face, thick and black, down his cheeks, from somewhere on his forehead to his jaw.

She said, 'No,' out loud. 'No, no,' but she couldn't move or shut the door. The man moved his head, and the stripes didn't move with it but dropped down on to the step and lay there in the sunshine. 'Kleenezee brushes,' he said, and stooped down to open the brown suitcase at his feet, and the bare branches of the clematis over the front door put their black shadows on his hand instead. 'Best quality brushes and brooms. I'd like you to see our new line. Scrubbing-brushes.'

He had a moustache. No paint. No stripes. Just a moustache.

'Twenty-two pence. The small ones are fourteen.'

'I'd like one of the small ones '

'Yes, madam. Thank you. No brooms today? Mops?'

'No, thank you. Not today.'

She went back into the kitchen.

'Post?' said Maureen.

'No, just a man.'

'What sort of a man?'

'A man with a striped face.'

'A *what*?'

'Never mind. Look, I've bought a scrubbing-brush.'

'Congratulations,' said Maureen.

There was something that had to be done. It was just a question of looking something up. Checking. Clare was well trained in looking things up. The aunts were great checkers. Dictionaries at Norham Gardens always lay open on tables, having just been used. Books had well-thumbed indexes. Always check your references, back your arguments with facts. Very well, then.

The picture was towards the end of the New Guinea book. She had marked it with a match. It was a black and white photograph, so there was no colour to help, and the line of shield-things that the men were holding was rather distant, but even so the pattern looked very like the pattern on that thing upstairs. And then there'd been something very similar in one of those old photos in the drawer of the desk in the drawing-room, she felt sure. To check properly, you needed to see all three together.

She spilled the photos out on to the desk. They were brown and yellow instead of black and white, and rather blurred. Evidently great-grandfather had not been an entirely successful photographer. Clare had looked at them before, but without great attention. Now she studied them carefully, one by one. They had writing on the back, she noticed for the first time. 'Cooke-Daniels exped. 1905' it said, on each, and then went on, more specifically, 'Sanderson, Hemmings, self, and porters' or 'Fly River Valley, Br. New Guinea'. Sanderson, Hemmings and self were all whiskery, stern-looking figures, dressed as though for a day on the grouse moors: the porters were naked except for a grass apron and half-moons of shell hung around their necks. The Fly River Valley was a smudgy brown pool in a darker brown bowl. She made a pile of the ones she had looked at: 'Tribesmen from Port Moresby area, Aug. 14th 1905' lined up as though for the end-of-year school photograph, but staring at the camera with eyes ringed in black dye, set in faces striped and etched, below elaborate, towering head-dresses: a single man with black eyebrows and a sad, wise face, feathers tucked in his hair—'Man from Quaipo tribe, useful informant on cannibal practices': children with pot bellies and spindly legs— 'Kamale boys immediately before initiation ceremony, men's house in background': a bearded man in plus-fours and tweed jacket between two dumpy, naked ladies with high mounds of black curly hair—'Self with women from Manumanu tribe'. And there at last was the one she had thought she remembered. A man, the usual aproned, shell-necklaced figure, stood by a blurry forest that she presently identified as bamboo: beyond him, half-hidden by one of his legs, was the shield thing. On the back, great-grandfather had written, 'Tribesman from interior with completed tamburan', and below that he had added, 'Specimen obtained for collection, Sept. 1905, excellent condition'.

Clare put the rest of the photographs back in the envelope. Then, with the book and the remaining photograph, she went up to the junk-room.

The first thing you noticed, going in there, always, was the smell. It was not unpleasant, not really a musty or stale smell, but somehow the smell of some other time, as though the air in the room, like the other things, was of 1890, or 1911, or 1926. Going into the room, it was you who became displaced in time: the room was quite at home. Clare picked up the slab of wood and carried it to the window to look at it carefully. The colours seemed to have got brighter since she had taken it out of the trunk—perhaps it was something to do with exposing it to the light. The reds were quite scarlet now, and the black very sharp, and the yellow very clear. Who had made it? Why? What would they feel about it being here, now, in an attic somewhere in the middle of England? She looked from the shield to the picture in the book and saw that the ones the men carried in that were not, after all, the same: similar, but not the same. She held the photograph to the light, and saw that in this case the pattern was identical—the circled eyes and swooping lines that made a thing that was both a pattern and the suggestion of human form. This was the one in the photograph, or, if not, another exactly the same. Once, a long time ago, this thing had stood by a plantation of bamboo, beyond the legs of a man wearing a half-moon of shell around his neck. He must be dead now, like great-grandfather.

She stood at the window, holding the shield and the photograph, looking from one to the other. Outside, a wind got up suddenly and made the telegraph wires, or the bare branches, sing with that odd noise she had heard before when she picked the Christmas roses, as though, far away, people were shouting.

Liz and Clare lay on their backs on Liz's bed, head to tail. Outside, lorries changed gear on Headington Hill, and the afternoon inched onwards.

'What's the time?'

'Guess.'

'Ten past three.'

'Not as good as that. Five past.'

'What shall we do?'

'Go out?'

'Too cold.'

'You always want it to be Saturday,' said Liz. 'And then when it is, it's dead boring.'

'Mmn.'

'My mum's always going on about how time flies. That's the last thing it does.'

'I know.'

'It's different for them, I s'pose.' Liz drew a hank of her own hair across her face and squinted into it. 'I've got split ends.'

'You can buy stuff in bottles to cure them. And depression and nerves and feeling tired in the morning.'

'I know,' Liz yawned. 'What we need is stuff in a bottle to make us about eighteen.'

'No.'

'Why not?'

'You'd go mad or something, if you suddenly woke up and found you were older.'

'I don't see why.'

'Because you wouldn't know what had happened in between— you can't manage unless you've got all that inside your head.'

'All right,' said Liz. 'If you say so. All the same, I wish I wasn't me now, if you see what I mean.'

They played cards, sitting cross-legged on the bed. Downstairs, Liz's mother clattered in the kitchen, busy, her time planned and allocated.

Aunt Anne came downstairs that evening, the first time for a week. She sat by the library fire in her chair and the room was once more properly furnished with aunts. Clare lay on the floor among ancient velvet cushions, icy draughts licking around her legs, and read. Aunt Anne was quiet, reading *The Times*, the same article again and again because she kept mixing the pages up. Aunt Susan was in one of her sharp moods, chatty, wanting to know things.

'Where did you go today?'

'To Headington. To Liz's house.'

'Liz. Let me see, now—round face and hair to the shoulder-blades?'

'No. That's Shelagh. Liz is thin face and long hair.'

'They all are prolific around the head. What did you do?'

'We were bored,' said Clare. 'Mostly.'

'Ah, that desperate boredom of youth. The everlasting after-noons. Almost a physical pain. One forgets what it felt like.'

'Were you and Aunt Anne bored?' said Clare, surprised.

'Frequently. We used to sit in the schoolroom *watching* the hands of the clock, screaming silently.'

'Where was everybody else?'

'The boys were away at school. Mamma would be out visiting. Father in his study. In any case, they would not have considered it their affair. Governesses were hired to deal with boredom.'

'Aunt Susan?'

'Yes dear?'

'Do you remember great-grandfather going on that expedition to New Guinea? The Cooke something expedition?'

'Not very well. I was only nine at the time. I remember that Mamma was very anxious, and much relieved when he returned. *The Times* did a series of articles about the expedition and of course father was much in demand as a lecturer. It was the basis for most of his future work, that expedition.'

'Yes. What happened to all the stuff he brought back?'

'It all went to the Pitt Rivers. It is a very important part of the collection.'

'All of it?'

'So far as I know.'

'There are still some things upstairs, in a trunk. Head-dresses, and arrows and that kind of thing.'

'Really,' said Aunt Susan. 'They must have been overlooked. Perhaps they were not of great interest. He did keep a small private collection, of course.'

'I think,' said Clare, 'that I might go to the Pitt Rivers tomorrow. I haven't been there for a long time.'

'That would be a good idea. I wish I could come with you, but my tiresome leg has been playing up again.'

If the Victorians can be said to have rampaged, they did so to greatest effect in the few acres of Oxford beside and immediately south of the University Parks. Stylistically, they achieved some of their most startling flights of fancy here. There is Keble College, red brick sprawling so copiously that one feels the stuff must have got out of control, unleashing some dark force upon a helpless architect. Or the houses that survive as tenacious Gothic islands amid the concrete cliffs of new University Departments—there seems to be something sinister at work here, some unquenchable life-force. Clare, cycling past in the teeth of a shrill wind, looked at them with the eye of a connoisseur, measuring their turrets and ecclesiastical front doors against her own. Not quite so good. If you believe in something, you should commit yourself up to the eyes, go the whole way.

They had gone the whole way with the Natural History Museum. Total commitment, unswerving belief. Here is a building dedicated to the pursuit of scientific truth built in a precise imitation of a church: how suitable that the debate on evolution should have taken place here, that Huxley should have confronted the bishops within these walls. Clare left the bicycle leaning against the railings. Some immense mining operation was going on next to the Museum, screened by fences: yellow bulldozers, manned by men in steel helmets, rumbled in and out, like a re-incarnation of the fossil dinosaurs within the museum. Perhaps the scientists, tired of expanding upwards, were retreating underground now, into subterranean laboratories. They want to be careful, she thought, around here. They don't know what they might stir up.

She went into the Museum with a feeling of coming home. It was a place she had always liked. It was like entering a Victorian station, St Pancras, or Euston: but a station furnished with fossils and pickled jellyfish and whale skeletons hung absurdly from the glass roof. There should be trains shunting, steam oozing around the gastropods and belemnites: instead there were flights of school-childern dashing from case to case, and students on camp-stools, drawing vertebrae and rib-cages. There was Prince Albert, in a marble frock-coat, presiding over pareisaurus and halitherium, all fossilised together, and there too were Galileo and Newton and Charles Darwin, five steps behind and slightly smaller, like figures on an Egyptian frieze, as befitted mere scientists, and commoners at that. Clare patted Prince Albert's foot and thought: when I'm seventeen, in about a hundred years' time, and I fall in love, I'll have assignations here. 'Meet you under the blue whale' I'll say, 'or by the iguanadon', and we'll melt at each other, like in old films, all among the invertebrates.

There was no time today, though, for the reproductive systems of squid, or the evolutionary process, or volcanic activity. She went through the doors at the far end, down the steps, and into the Pitt Rivers Museum, where the feeling of coming home was stronger still. The Indian totem towered over the central well of the place, all thirty-odd feet of it, managing somehow to retain a whiff of unfathomable mystery amid its surroundings of glass cases too close together and creaking floorboards. A memory of prairies and rivers and forests and mountains. If you wanted to be alone, the Pitt Rivers would always be a good place to come to: there would be three small boys staring respectfully at the shrunken heads, and a man in a dirty mac who looked as though he had strolled in from some seedy spy film, and the attendant, and nobody much else. You could wander alone and unremarked for hours among the stone axes and the Maori masks and the feathered head-dresses and shell necklaces. And the painted wooden shields.

There were three, she remembered, on the stairs. She went straight to them, and they were the same and yet not the same. The reds and the blacks and the yellows were there, and that distortion of human form, and the sense of a language so alien as to be impenetrable. Like a child's drawing of a man and yet, also, far more profound. Scientists, Clare remembered reading in a newspaper, had fired a rocket into outer space equipped, among other things, with a drawing of a naked man and woman, just in case there was something out there that might pick it up and wonder what kind of creature was responsible. It seemed touchingly optimistic: suppose the something thought only in terms of mathematics, or electronic communication, and was quite unfamiliar with the idea of a picture? And even if it recognised the symbolism, whatever would it think? These creatures are not very good artists. These creatures have no clothes. It would be as baffled as one felt here, up against processes of thought which were symbolic to an extent no one could follow, and yet were ancestral to one's own most basic instincts. Or so they said.

They were a different shape, too, these, and smaller, but certainly of the same family. They looked at her from the dark wall, projecting remote meanings, and told her nothing. One of them was labelled 'Carved and painted board, probably from one side of the entrance to the men's part of the Longhouse. Brit. New Guinea. Cooke-Daniels expedtn. dd. Major Cooke-Daniels 1905'. It wasn't the one in the photograph. Perhaps there were others elsewhere. She went up the stairs and creaked around the next gallery, among bone needles and spears and implements for making fire. No more wooden things.

She went down into the central hall again, and studied totems and wicker head-dresses and models of ships. And then she found another of the carved wooden things. It was in a case by itself, with a prim label saying that it was a war-shield, and the holes at the edges were probably for attaching the skulls of slaughtered enemies to. Very jolly. There, indeed, were the skulls. And it came from New Guinea, the label said, and was really very like the one in the attic, though again with small differences in the patterning. Clare had the feeling of being on the brink of understanding something. She went back to the ones on the stairs, and stared at them again.

Somebody came up the stairs, and stood beside her. She didn't turn, because she was busy looking.

Presently the person said, 'It's a fine collection they've got here. These ceremonial shields.'

'Yes. I s'pose so.'

'The African ones too are good. Are you studying shield-patterns? I saw you go from these to the others and then back. Looking at them for so long.'

He was tall and thin, all legs and arms, wearing jeans and a windcheater, with a file and some books under his arm. His voice was very deep and the English slightly accented, but not very, as though a long time ago he had spoken some other language.

Clare said, 'Not really. It's just I've got one at home.'

'That's a funny sort of thing to have at home.'

'It's a funny sort of home, I suppose.'

He laughed. A contagious laugh, from the stomach. She found herself smiling at him. He had very dark brown eyes, and a bloom on his black skin like the bloom on fruit, grapes or plums, as though he was exceptionally healthy.

'Not so funny. In my home we have ceremonial spears and my father's tribal dress, though he doesn't wear it any more.'

'It's funny for North Oxford,' said Clare. 'Where's your home?'

'Uganda. A little village one hundred miles from Kampala. John Sempebwa.' He held out his hand.

'I'm called Clare Mayfield.' They shook hands, John Sempebwa's enormous, quite engulfing hers. He laughed again, for no apparent reason.

'You're not a student, then?'

'I'm still at school,' said Clare.

'Excuse me, I thought you were older.'

Clare glowed. Older? Me? A student!

'I am studying anthropology,' he said. 'With Professor Sims.'

'My great-grandfather was an anthropologist. That's why we've got things like this at home. I say—I wonder—do you know anything about these things—these shields?'

He looked at the shield, and then at the label, and shook his head. 'It comes from New Guinea. I don't know anything about New Guinea. I am doing my thesis on witchcraft practice among the Baganda. I could tell you all about that. Or kinship structure. Would you like to hear about my relationship with my deceased aunt's husband?' Again the rich laugh. 'Excuse me, I forgot you were not an anthropologist. I am used to people asking me this kind of thing. Even the detribalised African can be useful, you see.'

'What's a detribalised African?'

'Me,' said John Sempebwa. This time Clare laughed, and he joined in. The attendant, parading the floor with clasped hands, looked disapproving.

'What is it you want to know about this thing?'

'I want to know what it means,' said Clare. Her voice came out very loud and abrupt.

Two schoolboys on the other side of the case stared at her. 'It's not just a thing, is it? Not like we have things—teapots or vases or book-ends. There's something else in it as well as what it looks like.'

'It's symbolic,' said John Sempebwa. 'This kind of thing is always symbolic. In Africa you get masks, costumes ... The patterns represent different tribes, and clans within the tribe, but more than that they are concerned with magical belief, that kind of thing. It is very complex, very difficult to understand. I couldn't tell you about these things, I'm afraid. What are they for, anyway?'

'The ones here are shields. Ceremonial shields. But mine is different. It's a different shape.'

'Perhaps you should bring it here? To show them?'

'Mmn. Perhaps.'

'You are worried by it, somehow?'

'Not really. Just—oh, just it bothers me a bit.' Knowing it's up there all the time. Like—like a letter you can't get open. Not understanding it.

'Things that are strange can be very puzzling,' said John. 'When

I first came to England I could not understand the underground system in London—red lines, black lines, Bakerloo, Northern line, Charing Cross, Earl's Court.' He laughed delightedly. 'I went round in circles, or in the wrong direction. Confusion! Then I saw it is all quite simple.'

'I hate it,' said Clare. 'All that hot wind.'

'Every face a strange one. Nobody knowing anybody else. That is alarming until you get used to it.'

The attendant was ringing a bell. 'This place closes at four,' said John. 'You have to leave your researches for another time.'

They walked together out of the Museum. Outside, the cold was like water: you walked into it as though into a tank and were immediately porous, icy trickles creeping under cuffs and collars, parting the hair, seeping through button-holes.

'I hate your winter,' said John. 'It gets into my soul.' He laughed. Laughter, for him, seemed not always to indicate amusement.

When they reached Clare's bike he held it for her to get on, flourishing it like a bouquet: Clare, unused to such gallantry, dropped her gloves in the mud. They scrabbled together to recover them.

'Which way are you going?' said John. He, too, had a bike.

'Norham Gardens.'

'May I ride so far with you? I go north too, but far north, beyond the roundabout.'

'Yes, please,' said Clare.

The wind was coming straight down from Iceland again, blowing smack at them so that they cycled as though trying to run up an escalator, losing as much ground as they gained. They had to turn their heads sideways to breathe, bawl at one another to be heard.

'What?'

'I said it's going to snow again. Have you many brothers and sisters?'

Clare shouted, 'No. I haven't got any parents. I live with my aunts. They're very old.'

'Cold?'

'OLD. Aunt Anne's seventy-eight and Aunt Susan's eighty.'

The wind dropped for a moment, deflected by a building, and John's voice came out loud and distinct. 'That must be good. To live with old people.'

'Yes. Yes, it is.'

'But here you do not respect old people as much as we do. In my country we admire the old. We take advice from them. Here it is the young who are admired.'

'Oh,' said Clare. 'Are they?'

'Of course. Haven't you noticed? They are made to feel important. Their opinions. What they say, what they want. You push your old people to one side. You let them be poor.'

They were going round into Norham Gardens now, and the dry hard wind was getting softer, and filling with snow. It drove into their faces, lay unmelting, in huge flakes, on John's black hair. To look up at the sky was to look into whirling confusion: the sky poured with snow.

John said, 'Is this what you call a blizzard?'

'I think so. This is where I live. Would you like to come and have tea with my aunts?'

CHAPTER 6

*The valley is a place without a past. The tribe do
not know how long they have been there: a hundred
years, a thousand, five thousand. Their future is
entrusted to the spirits of the ancestors, who care for
them and watch over them. One day, strangers come
to the valley and the tribe welcome them as these
spirits, returned with rich and wonderful gifts. They
are honoured, and given all they ask for.*

'Another cup, Mr Sempebwa?' said Aunt Susan.

John's large hand swamped the thin, cracked Crown Derby. He sat in front of the fire, his long legs folded like the limbs of a deck chair.

'Tell me, how do you think things are in Tanzania under this man Nyerere?' Aunt Susan was enjoying herself. She had become brisk, like she was five years ago. Tea had gone on for ages. John ate peanut butter sandwiches and two packets of digestive biscuits and talked about Africa, and Aunt Susan asked questions and made comments and poured tea. It was just like Aunt Susan, Clare thought, to be hopelessly muddled about money and forget what year it was and lose things all the time and yet to turn out to know all about what happened in Kenya last month or what the Prime Minister of Uganda was called. That was the aunts all over.

At last John said he must go. In the hall, putting on his coat, he said, 'Your aunt is a very well-informed lady.'

'Yes. It's just everyday things she's a bit vague about. Gutters, and things like that.'

'Gutters?'

'You know—the things round the top of a house to catch the rain. They're very expensive to get mended.'

'Most schoolgirls wouldn't know about that kind of thing.'

'I'm a detribalised schoolgirl.'

John's laughter brought Maureen out of her room, peering down the well of the staircase.

'Would you like me to look at this New Guinea shield of yours before I go?' he said. 'Then I could perhaps look it up in the anthropology library and let you know about it.'

'Yes, please.'

Up in the attic, he was astonished. 'What's this?'

'A linen press. You put sheets and things in it and screw it up and it squashes them flat.'

'And that?'

'A gramophone. With a loudspeaker. It doesn't work.'

'It is certainly of historic interest,' said John politely. 'This is your shield?'

'Yes. Only it's not a shield.'

He studied it. 'I can remember the design. I am trained for remembering that kind of thing. I'll look it up.'

'Thanks.'

They went downstairs again. Maureen's door opened, and closed.

'Goodbye. Thank you for inviting me to tea.'

'I'm afraid it wasn't very posh.'

'It was very nice. I liked meeting your aunt.'

Outside the snow still came down in wild confusion, picked out by the street lamps. It defied gravity, snowing from right to left in front of the house, and ten yards back from left to right. Beyond the garden well it spouted upwards, snowing in reverse.

'Christ!' said John. 'Excuse me.' He swamped his head and shoulders in a huge striped scarf, and got on to the bike. 'Goodbye.'

'Goodbye,' said Clare. She watched him go into the darkness, heading north, his raincoat flapping over the back wheel of the bicycle, and closed the front door.

'I saw your friend,' said Maureen. 'The foreign one.'

'Oh.'

'It's interesting,' said Maureen, 'getting to know foreign people. We had a German girl in the office once. Mind, that's not quite the same. Known him a long time, have you?'

'About half an hour, when you saw him. We picked each other up, I think.'

'Well!' said Maureen. 'I wouldn't have thought you'd do that. Did you go to the pictures on your own, then?'

'It wasn't the pictures. It was in a museum.'

Maureen reflected. 'I suppose you'd get a different type in a museum. All the same, I wouldn't think your aunts would fancy that kind of thing.' Severely.

'Oh, they did. Aunt Susan gave him three cups of tea and talked to him for nearly three hours.'

'Well!' said Maureen again.

The blizzard roared all that night. The Norham Gardens houses stood four-square against it like battleships and it screamed against the brick and threw tiles down on to cars and tarmac and snapped branches from the trees. And then it raged away south, leaving one side of each building furred over with driven snow. Tongues of snow licked up the sides of fences: each sill and gutter was laden. The postman posted snow through the front door with the letters. The wireless dwelt on traffic chaos, stranded snow-ploughs and helicopters raining hay upon Exmoor to hungry sheep.

The letters, damp and blotched, were a brochure from a travel firm and a postcard from cousin Margaret in Norfolk. The travel firm wanted the aunts to enjoy a fun-packed fortnight on the fabulous Costa del Sol: cousin Margaret, on the other side of a photograph of Norwich cathedral, hoped they were all surviving this foul weather and would like to pop down to see them on Monday night, between the dentist and a school play. Uncle Edwin sent his love and would they forgive the scrawl, everything being a mad rush as usual. Tonight that was. Oh, dear. Clare put the Costa del Sol in the wastepaper basket, and propped cousin Margaret's card on the kitchen mantelpiece. Doing so reminded her of Mrs Hedges' tonic. She took an extra large spoonful. It felt like the kind of day on which one might need hidden resources.

She'd slept badly, too. Blizzards, disintegrating bedclothes, and other things.

The spare room would need to be tidied out for cousin Margaret. She'd have to leave a note for Mrs Hedges. It was unlike cousin Margaret to make a sortie from Norfolk in mid-winter. In fact, come to think of it, one couldn't remember ever having seen cousin Margaret out of summer. August, windy beach picnics, jam-making, wasps, thunderstorms: that was cousin Margaret's rightful background. It seemed inappropriate that she should turn out to have a mobile, winter existence as well. In between summer visits to Norfolk, Clare realised guiltily, she hardly ever thought of cousin Margaret and cousin Edwin and all the little cousins, and their large scruffy house and weedy tennis court and their cosy, faintly excluding family life. They were a family in which everyone had nicknames, and in which conversations took place in a private jargon that had to be de-coded, with amiable con-descension, for visitors. One was forever tripping over one's own mistakes—not knowing the code word for areas of house or garden, or ignorant of some custom or ritual, being put right by kindly six-year-olds, amazed at the ignorance of outsiders. How did they manage, the little cousins, beyond the confines of the family? Or did they colonise, so to speak—establish extensions in the outside world, make conversions, baptise into the faith? Converts, though, like visitors, would always be kept conscious of their position as temporary, courtesy members of the family—not of the blood. And how did cousin Margaret manage, on expeditions like this, adrift from her anchorage? It was impossible to imagine: cousin Margaret seemed an undetachable part of her own house, as integral as the smell of cooking, children and dogs.

Clare left a note for Mrs Hedges explaining about cousin Margaret. The aunts were not up yet, so she explained to Aunt Susan, who seemed pleased at the idea of a visitor, through the bedroom door. Then she went out into cold, storm-battered streets, and to school.

On the way home it occurred to her that cousin Margaret should perhaps be treated to something more elaborate than soup and scrambled egg. Much eating was done in Norfolk: huge stews, joints, puddings. Well, Norham Gardens couldn't rise to that, but chops would not be unmanageable.

She had to wait in the butcher's, standing in a line of muffled ladies, hunched against the cold, staring at bright lights and meat. The shop glowed with meat: dark drums of beef, rosy pork, skeins of pink sausages that delicately brushed the butcher's head as he reached into the window. Somebody here had an eye for style. The window display was ready to be painted, a mortuary still-life, cutlets fanned out seductively, edged with plastic parsley, spare ribs flaring in a circle, steaks lined up with military precision. The butcher was a huge man, his self-confidence as hard as a rock. He brandished cleavers and juggled with knives, at the other end of the counter his assistant clubbed unresisting steak: jokes flew between them over the heads of the customers. The customers were sheep, only one rung up from the meat. The butcher patronised them. 'Next young lady?' he roared, and the middle-aged housewives shuffled forward, obediently amused. 'Now then, what's for you today, and how's your old man?' Behind him the pig carcases hung from hooks, as docile as the customers.

'Next, please? Yes, my love?'

Clare pointed to the pink and white fan of chops. 'Four, please.'

'Two for you and two for him. Dinner for the boy friend, is it?' A mammoth wink.

Clare shrank into her coat. Snails must feel like that, pinned down by the blackbird's steely eye.

Everybody was staring at her. The neat pig-halves and divided sheep swivelled on their hooks to get a better look.

'What's his name then? Who's the lucky fellow?' Stab! went the blackbird's yellow beak. Thump! the butcher's cleaver, splitting bone.

'How much is that, please?'

'Forty-four to you. And give him my compliments.' The snail, wincing, glowing pink, crawled out, forgot her purse, had to go back, spotlit by eight pairs of eyes, fell over someone's foot, got stabbed again, escaped.

Outside, Liz was stowing library books into a bike basket. 'What's the matter?'

'I've just become a vegetarian.'

'Oh. Why? Listen—come down into the town with me.'

'No. I can't. I've got cousin Margaret.'

'You make her sound like a disease.'

'She might be,' said Clare. Liz went away into the dusk, swallowed up among the cars.

Back at Norham Gardens the aunts, of course, had forgotten all about cousin Margaret. Aunt Anne had been feeling poorly again and had gone back to bed. Aunt Susan, in front of a waning fire, was sitting surrounded by brown cardboard boxes from which spilled pamphlets and yellowing papers.

'Is that you, dear? I am having a tidy-up. Do you know that in 1932 Anne and I went to nineteen committee meetings and lobbied our M.P. four times? He was a tedious man, I remember. And we marched from Hyde Park Corner to Trafalgar Square, about unemployment. Here is a photograph in *The Times*.'

'Which is you?'

'The second blur from the left, I rather think.'

'It doesn't do you justice,' said Clare. 'Cousin Margaret will be here tonight.'

'So she will. How nice. We had better eat in the dining-room. I wonder if you would mind fetching my thick tweed coat from upstairs.'

'I've got some chops. Why are butchers such noisy men?'

'I suppose it's a job that blunts the sensibilities.'

'Bossy too.'

'A legacy from the war. They wielded enormous power. People would suffer any humiliation for a pound of offal or a sausage.'

Clare banked up the fire, and cleared bundles of letters and papers from one of the chairs, in anticipation of cousin Margaret. The tidy-up was having the effect of slowly engulfing the room in paper and newsprint. Aunt Susan was having a lovely time: she drifted from her chair to the bookshelves and back, disembowelling files and boxes.

'Dear me, here are all my old lecture notes. And Anne's

correspondence with the Webbs. How interesting.'

Cousin Margaret arrived by taxi off the London train at half past six. Her travelling, and winter, persona differed from the static summer one only in being embellished with a hat, uncomfortable shoes, and dabs of powder and lipstick.

'Lovely to see you, Clare dear. How are the aunts? Goodness, I'd forgotten what a morgue this place is. What a pity they can't move into something smaller.'

They went upstairs. 'How's school? Everything going all right? Bumpy and Sue-Sue sent their love—the big ones are all back at school, of course. I've just been down for the play, you know, that's why I'm here, really. And of course I wanted to see you and the aunts.' Cousin Margaret stripped herself of hat and coat and vanished into the bathroom. Above vigorous sounds of washing came more news of cousin Edwin, children, the school play, the Christmas holidays.

'... so with Dodie and the Sprockets we were fourteen for dinner, and then we all played charades in the dark. You must come, another Christmas, Clare—I don't like to think of you being dull here with the aunts. What? Oh well, that's fine, then. I just thought it might be all a bit *elderly* for you. They're a bit out of touch now, aren't they, poor dears.'

They visited Aunt Anne, in bed. More news, more names. Visits to pantomimes in Norwich, school prize-givings, village concerts. Aunt Anne smiled, bewildered. 'Tell me,' said cousin Margaret, going downstairs, 'how *is* she? I thought she was rather quiet.'

'The doctor came. He said it wasn't anything to worry about.'

'Of course she is seventy-seven. Or is it seventy-eight?'

In the library, Aunt Susan had recaptured the other chair. She beamed happily from a sea of old envelopes.

'Goodness!' said cousin Margaret. 'You could do with a proper spring-clean in here. You must let me give you a hand. I love throwing things away. How are you, Aunt Susan?'

They kissed. Cousin Margaret sat down. 'Lovely to see you all looking so well. Well, you'll be wanting to hear all our news. Oh, Clare, I meant to tell you—poor Wooffy did die. We were afraid she was going to.'

Wooffy? Dog? Cat? Or the old nurse?

'So we got a new little bitch right away. I didn't want the children to get morbid about it.'

Must be the dog. Hope so, anyway. 'I'm so sorry,' said Clare. 'How sad.'

'Do you know, Margaret,' said Aunt Susan, 'I have just come across a whole lot of old letters from Beatrice and Sydney Webb. We served on a committee with them once, you know. Do you remember meeting them here when you were a small girl?'

Cousin Margaret spread plump legs to the fire.

'I can't say I do, Aunt Susan. There were always such a lot of odd bods around in the old days, weren't there? Oh—and we had another tragedy. Mr Patcham got into a fight in the village and we had to have him put to sleep.'

Aunt Susan looked startled.

'He was dreadfully bitten. It must have been that horrid tom from the pub. One does go through such anguish with animals. Sue-Sue cried for days.'

'Would you like a glass of sherry, cousin Margaret?' said Clare. 'My dear, I should love one.'

The sherry, sandwiched between copies of *Hansard*, had not been opened, to Clare's certain knowledge, for over five years, but cousin Margaret drank it with gusto. Maybe it was stuff that improved with age.

Aunt Susan said, 'Clare is a pillar of support these days. I don't know what we should do without her.'

'Oh, good,' said cousin Margaret. 'Splendid. I had wondered, if perhaps ... Never mind. I say, I *wish* you could see Bumpy—he's lost both his front teeth. He looks a perfect scream.'

Aunt Susan nodded and smiled. She was beginning to look quenched by all this information. The papers and envelopes made drifts around her feet, stirring sometimes in response to draughts from the chimney. Cousin Margaret gulped sherry and handed out news: cousin Edwin had a filthy cold, poor darling, council houses were to be built on the church field, Sue-Sue was growing plaits, there had been a *coup d'état* in the Women's Institute.

'And what about you, Clare dear? I want to hear everything

you've been doing. By the way, we're expecting you in August—you will be coming, won't you?'

'Yes, please,' said Clare. 'Thank you very much.'

'They are very pleased with Clare at school,' said Aunt Susan. 'We hear very good reports.'

'Oh well, I expect she's got the family brains. Lucky girl. But you mustn't just swot, Clare dear—people get so narrow-minded like that, don't they? Oh—did I tell you Sal's going to France for a year when she leaves school? It would sort of open her out, we thought. To a family.'

'A family?' said Clare.

'Yes. In the country. Six children, and lots of animals and things. It sounds lovely.'

'I expect she'll love it. Being opened out in a family.'

Something slipped off Aunt Susan's lap. Clare picked it up. 'What's this, Aunt Susan?'

'Oh, I was going to show you. It's part of the diary father kept in New Guinea. On the expedition, you know. The other volumes seem to have got lost, but I came across this one, and I thought it might interest you.'

Brown, loopy handwriting. Crossings-out. A squashed insect between two of the pages. 'Yes. Yes, I'd like to read it very much. In fact I'd love to.'

'Clare was looking at things father gave to the Pitt Rivers,' said Aunt Susan. 'She brought back a most interesting young man. An African. We had such a pleasant talk.'

'Sue-Sue loves museums,' said cousin Margaret. 'We took her to the V. and A. you know, last holidays, and she was so funny. Do you know what she said? She was looking at the costumes and . . .'

Clare got up, stealthily, and backed out of the room. The flow did not abate. It seemed mean, leaving Aunt Susan defenceless like that, but then she did have a capacity for just shutting herself off if the turn of events was unpromising, and would no doubt do so now. She went into the kitchen, where the chops lay inert upon the table. Right, then, let's be having you. Next young lady please, and how's your father?

They ate in the dining-room. Great-grandfather and great-grandmother presided, remote behind the glass of their portraits. Great-grandmother, in red silk to the floor, most elegantly curved fore and aft, leaned against a marble pillar and contemplated an ostrich feather fan. Great-grandfather, stern and whiskered, sat with open book (no, volume) upon his knee, deep in thought (back in the Fly River valley, perhaps, with Sanderson and Hemmings?).

'Wasn't she gorgeous?' said cousin Margaret. 'Aunt Violet. It's Sargent, isn't it, that portrait? Jolly good chops, I must say.'

Aunt Susan looked over the top of her spectacles at the portrait: the positions seemed reversed, juggled about by time, she the mother, the young woman in the red dress the daughter. 'Yes. It was exhibited at the Royal Academy, I remember. Poor father was made to go to the opening view. Not the kind of occasion he cared for at all.'

'That dress is in one of the trunks in the attic,' said Clare.

'All mother's things were kept.'

'That I cannot understand,' said cousin Margaret, helping to clear away. 'The way they've never ever thrown away a single thing. It's stuffed, this place, like a museum.' The baize door bumped softly behind them as they went through to the kitchen. 'Heavens, Clare, how do you manage with that stove? And the sink!'

'They're all right if you're used to them.'

'I couldn't live without my Aga. Shall I wash, and you put away?'

'Thank you.'

'There was something I rather wanted to talk to you about.' Cousin Margaret ran water on to the plates, swabbing with practised energy. 'Just while we've got the chance.'

'Yes?'

'It's just that you're always welcome, you know, at Swaffham. You must feel you can always come to us. As family, you know. Edwin and I did want you to be sure about that.'

'In August?'

'Actually I meant any time. If anything happened, you know.'

'If anything happened?'

'Yes.' Water spat from the tap, spun off the plates. 'Eventually.'

Eventually. Quite a few. When your mum and dad—er. 'Do you mean,' said Clare, 'if the aunts died?'

Cousin Margaret turned the tap on violently. Above rushing water and clatter she could be heard to say things about how of course one didn't, and naturally one hoped, and there was no reason to.

'Thank you,' said Clare. 'It's very kind of you and cousin Edwin. Very kind.'

'And of course it is such fun for the young down there. You know—the Pony Club and the Young Farmers and all that.'

'Yes.'

'Sal has a marvellous time in the holidays.'

'Yes.'

'Hunt Balls, in a year or two. We do feel it must be a bit dull for you here.'

'Actually,' said Clare, 'it isn't dull at all. I like this house being cold and dusty and peculiar and I think the aunts are the most interesting people I've ever known. If they are out of touch, like you said, then I think I'd rather be too, if being in touch is what I think it is. I've always liked living with them and I wouldn't like to live anywhere else. When you talk to the aunts they listen, and I listen back at them. The only thing that's wrong is that they're old, and as a matter of fact I don't see what's wrong with that anyway.' She dropped a plate: it smacked down on to the floor and lay in three neat pieces.

Cousin Margaret blinked. She stared at the plug and said, 'Yes. Quite. Yes, I do see what you mean.'

Clare picked up the bits of plate, looked at them, and put them in the dustbin.

'We keep breaking things these days,' she said. 'Maureen broke one of these the other day.'

'Maureen?' said cousin Margaret, brightly.

'She's somebody who lives here now. In one of the top rooms. We had a Gap—I mean a financial problem—so I decided to let one of the rooms. Mrs Hedges got it ready and I found Maureen in the Post Office window.'

Cousin Margaret blinked again. She wiped her hands on the

kitchen towel and said, 'Well, I must say, you do seem awfully sensible about things, Clare.'

'Oh,' said Clare. 'Good.'

'I wouldn't have thought the aunts would have been all that keen on the idea of a lodger, that's all.'

'They don't mind.'

'Don't they? Oh, I see. Perhaps we'd better go through and join Aunt Susan?'

'Yes,' said Clare. They went through the baize door again. In the hall cousin Margaret stopped in front of the mirror and prodded her hair. She was looking very pink. 'I must say,' she said, 'you do seem to cope awfully well. I sometimes wonder if perhaps Sal is a bit ... Of course, being one of a large family is marvellous, but ... Oh well. But, Clare, do get in touch if ever, well, if ever you have any problems.'

'Yes,' said Clare, 'I'll get in touch. Thank you, cousin Margaret. Thanks very much.'

Later, lying in bed, with the house huge and silent around her, everyone stowed away into separate rooms, the aunts, Maureen, cousin Margaret having a bath, with sounds of distant splashing, she opened the diary and began to read.

'Aug. 10th 1905. Port Moresby. This morning we reached the settlement here, which is the seat of our Administration, and are lodged, as comfortably as one might expect, at the Residency. One cannot but admire the efforts of the Administrator to bring the advantages of British justice to the natives of Papua, beset as he is on all sides by difficulties, not least of which is the lack of co-operation of the tribes who are in a state of constant tumultuous warfare with each other, and who indulge in headhunting and cannibalism. Their chief intercourse with Europeans has been hitherto with missionaries, several of whom, I am informed, have met with a fate upon which it is pleasanter not to dwell. The heat is great, and the insects a torment. Sanderson and Hemmings are anxious to depart as soon as possible for the interior. A letter awaited me here from Violet, who writes that Eights Week was most agreeable, in good weather, with Christ Church head of the river. Little Susan wrote too, in a good firm hand, and a nice attention to spelling.'

There was a blob of wax on the page at this point, as though great-grandfather had tipped the candle over. The next entry was nearly a week later.

'Aug. 16th. We have spent several days now in exploration of the Kemp-Welch basin, having secured the services of porters in Port Moresby, as well as the protection of some native police, most kindly supplied by the Administrator, and for whose presence we have indeed been grateful, the massacre of unwary travellers being apparently common in these parts. The terrain is most inhospitable and we advance but a few miles each day, being impeded by the luxuriance of the vegetation, which consists for the most part of dense forests of eucalyptus, mangrove swamps, and plantations of bamboo, pandanus and sugar-cane around the native villages. The tribes in this part are the Kamale, Quaipo, and Veiburi, and are extremely unwilling to enter into friendly intercourse—I have met with great difficulty in persuading them to talk. However, some men of the Veiburi tribe were more forthcoming than most and with the aid of an interpreter I was able to make some useful notes about burial customs, taboos and spiritual beliefs. Hemmings has some fine bird of paradise skins, and Sanderson is well pleased with his botanical specimens. I have obtained some good examples of the stone adzes used by these tribesmen, and am most anxious to secure further items, in particular the ceremonial masks and shields of which I have heard, and of which the finest, I believe, are to be found in the Purari River area.'

At this point a half page had been left blank, to accommodate an insect, squashed and unidentifiable. Had it tormented great-grandfather and been summarily dealt with?

The diary proceeded. Sometimes the entries were long and detailed, sometimes brief, a mere few words noting the position, or date, as though great-grandfather had been too exhausted after a day contending with mangrove swamps and native hostility to do more than flop on to his camp bed. Hemmings developed a fever, and they had to halt for several days on the coast, where great-grandfather busied himself collecting accounts of tribal superstition.

'These are a people deeply imbued with spiritual beliefs,' he wrote. 'For them the invisible world is as real as the visible, believing as they do that all living creatures possess souls and spirits, which, after leaving the mortal frame, wander hither and thither during the hours of the night. So easy and unaffected is their converse with spirits, in particular the spirits of their ancestors, that to become for long involved with their ways of thought is to feel one's own rational foundations begin to shake. The world of scientific truth seems at times as remote as my own study in Norham Gardens.' Hemmings recovered, though the poor fellow had lost much weight and was a dreadful yellow colour, and the party embarked in a small steamship for the Fly River where they spent a few days chugging along the swampy river, largely for the benefit of Sanderson, who wished to make a collection of the orchids and creepers that grew on the banks. Any natives that were to be found fled in confusion on sight of the steamship, or rained arrows upon them from the shelter of the undergrowth so that great-grandfather was under-occupied and spent the time organising his notes and complaining of the humidity. The high point of the expedition, for him, was yet to come.

The party left the Fly River and made their way to the delta of the Purari. This was the moment for which great-grandfather had been waiting. 'At last,' he wrote, 'I approach the principal of my objectives, namely the acquisition of one of the fine ceremonial shields manufactured by the tribes of this area. Similar to those brought out of the Sepik River valley by Herr Muller, and which I have been shown in Hamburg, they are known as tamburans, or kwoi, and play a crucial role in the spiritual life of their makers.' The Purari river proved even more uncomfortable than the Fly, hot and swampy, and obscured most of the time by dense curtains of mist (which reminded great-grandfather of family holidays on the west coast of Scotland). The small steamer kept going aground, so that they were obliged to get out and make their way along the bank. 'It is the most unpleasant walking,' said great-grandfather, with some understatement. 'Beset as we are by such hazards as snakes and black leeches which fasten themselves upon the skin and suck blood until they are detached, when festering sores almost invariably ensue. At times we are driven to walk in the river itself, in which there are alligators.'

However, after a few days of this, they reached more open country, and the foothills of the mountainous interior, beyond which lay huge unexplored tracts of land. They began to climb. Great-grandfather described graphically the long haul through dripping rain-forests, and their relief as they reached the summit of the mountain ridge and found beyond a wide and pleasant valley. And here, at last, were the native settlements they had been expecting, the remote and isolated peoples never before encountered by Europeans.

Great-grandfather was excited and impressed.

'Our first contact with the inhabitants came at mid-day today. We approached a small settlement of grass-thatched huts and as we did so a detachment of male tribesmen came forward to meet us. They were naked except for a posterior pendant of grass, a marine shell of a half-moon shape suspended from the neck, and ornaments of cassowary and bird-of-paradise plumes in the hair. Their faces were most wonderfully painted and decorated. Observing them to be armed with bows and arrows as well as spears, and indeed, to be about to fire upon us, we shouted and waved, attempting to indicate that our intentions were friendly. As we drew nearer, they lowered their weapons, and began to chatter and exclaim among themselves with much wonder and astonishment. They allowed us to come up to them, whereupon they touched our faces and hair with much amazement, as though they could hardly believe that we were flesh and blood. Our clothes, too, astonished them, and our equipment—they gathered around us, touching and examining, expressing their wonder and surprise with small clicking noises of the tongue. All hostility seemed to have evaporated.

And then, with great excitement, I perceived the very thing I was so anxious to acquire. A little way apart from the other huts stood a rather larger structure, and there at either side of the entrance were three or four examples of the ceremonial shields, hung upon the walls. We were all struck at once by the power and presence of these objects, and indeed with their not inconsiderable artistic merit. Brilliantly coloured, in red, black and yellow, they have a patterning which is undoubtedly of an anthropomorphic nature. It seems possible that they were originally images of the ancestors, and retain some kind of precious symbolism, the exact nature of which it is hard to ascertain. We expressed our desire to examine the shields more closely, which, with some little reluctance they allowed. Finally I could contain myself no longer, and, with the aid of my interpreter, explained my wish to possess one of the shields, offering in exchange anything they wished in the usual currency of tobacco, beads and cloth.

This threw them into some confusion: they seemed, while unwilling at first to comply, to feel that they might not refuse, and after more discussion they allowed me to select one of the tamburans. We camped that night in the village and were treated with great ceremony and deference, almost, it seemed, as though we were members of the tribe. In the morning, as we prepared ourselves to continue our journey, the leaders came to us and said farewell with great solemnity, assuring us that we should see them again, and once more wondering at our possessions and asking us to send them such things for their own use. Indeed, it was a strange and touching thing to have witnessed the first contact between a savage people and the representatives of western culture: we went on our way much impressed by the encounter and pleased with our kindly reception, so unlike the naked hostility usually met with among the tribes of New Guinea.'

It was late. The hall clock chimed twelve. The house was quite quiet now, and the street outside. New Guinea was the other side of the world: great-grandfather had died nearly forty years ago.

Clare turned out the light and lay staring at the ceiling for what seemed a long time. She heard the hall clock strike one, and must have fallen asleep soon after because when, later, she woke again her watch said ten past two. In the interval she had dreamed, and for a moment, in a half-awake state, confused the dream for reality. She had got out of bed, she thought, just before, because it seemed to her that the house was in some way disturbed, not by noise but a strange intensity of feeling. Her watch had stopped, and so had the hall clock—indeed the silence, as she went downstairs, was insistent. She stood in the hall for a moment, and as she did so the dining-room door opened—of its own accord it seemed—and there was great-grandfather, standing by the sideboard looking out of the window. Behind him, the tamburan was propped against the wall. The portrait of great-grandfather had gone: there was a whitened patch on the wallpaper where it should have been. Great-grandfather looked towards Clare—she noticed what a worried expression he had, and how his beard was yellower at one side than the other (she thought, in a detached way, that this must be something to do with smoking a pipe, and the angle at which he smoked it). He drew the curtain, and now Clare could hear a noise from somewhere outside—shrill, high-pitched chanting or singing—and she saw that the brown people were out there again, lots of them. Great-grandfather looked out at them, and seemed to say something. The dream ended, and Clare, waking abruptly, took several moments to re-adjust herself, lying in the darkness listening to a car in the street outside, to the wind rattling the window, to the clocks.

CHAPTER 7

The tribe work in their gardens, shelter from the rain, eat, sleep, are born, grow up, and die. They talk to the ancestors, and remind them that they await a share of the riches they now enjoy, up there beyond the clouds. The ancestors are benevolent, and will provide.

'You look peaky, my dear,' said cousin Margaret, having a good breakfast before the journey home. 'You ought to have a better colour, at your age.'

Snow dislodged itself from the gutter, and flopped past the kitchen window.

'Plenty of fresh air.'

'Yes,' said Clare.

'And lots of sleep. Eight hours at least.'

'Perhaps that's what it is.'

'Well, I must press on.' Cousin Margaret gathered herself, checked train tickets, purse, gloves. 'I'll just pop up and say goodbye to the aunts.'

On the stairs cousin Margaret and Maureen passed each other, said 'Good morning' brightly, and examined one another without turning their heads, eyes slanted sideways. Maureen went out into the street and cousin Margaret could be heard upstairs, whisking round the aunts like an amiable wind, set on a course that allowed for no deflection. She came down, carrying a suitcase that leaked a yard or so of dressing-gown cord.

'Well, goodbye, my dear. We'll see you in August, then?'

'Yes,' said Clare.

'And I hope Aunt Anne's cold clears up.'

'So do I.'

'Oh, of course it will. A day or two in bed ...'

'Give my love to Uncle Edwin.'

'Yes. Keep in touch, won't you? Have a lovely holidays, when they come. I must rush, or I'll miss the train.'

Clare, wheeling her bike out of the drive, saw cousin Margaret turn the corner into Banbury Road, a confident figure bundled into coat and hat, bolstered with unswerving convictions that all was well with the world, whatever anyone might say to the contrary. A bus loomed in the grey morning light, and cousin Margaret broke into a trot and vanished, the dressing-gown cord leaving a thin line behind her on the snowy pavement. Clare got on to her bike and headed north.

She was doing homework in the kitchen when the doorbell rang. It was John Sempebwa.

'Hello.'

'Hello. Is this a convenient time to call? I found out something about your shield.'

She took him into the kitchen. 'Sorry about the mess.'

'Not at all,' said John. 'It is homely.' He pulled a chair out from the table and sat down. 'What are you writing?'

'An essay on the causes of the Civil War. It's my history homework.'

'Do you like history?'

'Yes. There's so much of it, though. To get straight about. What comes when.'

'That's because you live in a country with a lot to remember.'

'Oh,' said Clare. 'Is that a good thing?'

'It must be. New countries look for historians before they look for doctors or tax collectors. Let me tell you what I've found out for you.' He took a notepad out of his pocket. Clare hooked her feet over the rung of her chair and leaned forward a little.

'It's something called a tamburan, or a kwoi in some parts of New Guinea. It doesn't have anything to do with fighting—it's a ceremonial shield. They used to make them and then hang them in a place called the men's house which each village had, all around the walls.'

'Like family portraits,' said Clare.

John laughed. 'In a way. The same idea, certainly. Continuity. Preserving the life of the tribe. They are symbolic, of course, like I thought, but no one seems very clear about what the patterns mean. The article I read said "From several considerations, especially from their anthropomorphic nature, it appears possible that they were originally images of ancestors". Anthropomorphic means ...'

'I know,' said Clare, 'like people.' Circles for eyes, a kind of mouth ...

'Sorry. I'm sounding like a schoolmaster.'

'It's just that I've been reading a book about New Guinea, and that word came in, but it didn't really say anything about the shields —the tamburans—but it did have a picture of some rather the same.'

'So now you know what it is you have upstairs,' said John. 'Quite interesting. You should take good care of it—there aren't many around, this article said, except the ones in the Pitt Rivers and a few in museums in Australia and New Guinea. They used to set a lot of value on them, the tribes, because of what they represent, and they weren't keen on letting anyone have them.'

'My great-grandfather got this one. From a tribe who'd never seen European people before.'

'Clever gentleman. How did he persuade them to give it to him?'

'I'm not sure really. I think they didn't quite understand who he was. Him and Sanderson and Hemmings.'

'Perhaps you should take the one upstairs along to the Pitt Rivers. It's obviously important, from an ethnological point of view.'

'I think they want it back,' said Clare.

'I thought you'd always had it here. Upstairs.'

'Not them meaning the Pitt Rivers. Them. The people who made it.'

John looked bewildered.

'Never mind. It doesn't matter. Do you know—in this book I've been reading it says they've still been finding new tribes right up till a few years ago, in remote valleys where nobody'd ever been. Tens of thousands of people nobody'd known existed, just living there sort of in the Stone Age still, not knowing anything about the rest of the world.'

'I shouldn't think it's very nice when they find out.'

'No. They get diseases they hadn't had before and want things they didn't know they wanted and some of them go kind of mad. It's very sad, reading about it.'

'Cultural disintegration,' said John.

'What?'

'Something that happens to people if you suddenly destroy their traditional way of life. They can't cope.'

'The trouble was,' said Clare, 'the old way was awful too. They were all killing each other all the time. You can see they couldn't let that go on, the people who found them.'

'Exactly. Very difficult. There was an article about that problem too in the library. About them expecting the ancestors to come back to them in aeroplanes, bringing riches. They stop making tamburans, by the way, as soon as they've jumped into the twentieth century like this. They seem to forget how, or why they did it.'

The kitchen clock whirred and clicked and struck six. 'Excuse me,' said John, 'I must go. I'm room-hunting. I've missed two today already and I've heard of one in Park Town. If I don't hurry someone will take it before I get there.'

'I thought you lived beyond the roundabout?'

'I did. My landlady gave me notice. I have to go next week. Well, goodbye.'

'Hang on ...' said Clare.

'What?'

'Just hang on one minute. I have to ask the aunts something.'

'All right—but I must go. Give my regards to your aunts.'

She went out into the hall, the baize doors swinging behind her, and into the library before she could give herself time to think of should I? or what would they say? or shall I?

'Aunt Susan?'

'Yes, dear.'

'Do you remember John who came to tea the other day?'

'Certainly.'

'Could he come and live here?'

Aunt Susan let her glasses slide an inch or two down her nose, and laid down the newspaper she was reading. 'Has he nowhere to live?'

'Not from next week. His landlady gave him notice. And we've got nineteen rooms.'

'Have we really?' said Aunt Susan. 'Yes, I suppose we have. Another lodger? Mother would have been appalled. Absolutely appalled.'

'Please.'

'I would have liked to see what Anne thought, but she is having a nap, and in any case I don't want to worry her with things at the moment.'

'He wouldn't be any bother. I know he wouldn't.'

'Well,' said Aunt Susan, 'all things considered, I don't think we can do otherwise. But tell him the room is free.'

'No. He wouldn't come if we did that.'

Aunt Susan looked at her. 'Possibly you're right. Ten shillings a week, then, do you think that would be too much?'

'No. Thanks, Aunt Susan. See you in a minute.'

'Well!' said Mrs Hedges. 'It's getting to be a proper guest-house, isn't it? How much are you asking him?'

'Three-fifty, same as Maureen. It couldn't be less, or she'd have minded if she found out.'

Mrs Hedges nodded. 'That'll take care of the builder's bill, in a week or two.'

'He's not really part of the gap,' said Clare. 'He's a friend, more.'

'Still, it all comes in handy. That little room at the back, on the second floor, would be best, I should think.'

Great-grandmother's writing-room, it had been once, and the function had survived thereafter, in the name. 'Mother's writing-room', the aunts had always called it, though it had for far longer housed junk, relations, refugees from Germany before the war, and now, old newspapers. Clare pulled a pile of them out of a cupboard and read headlines about Korea and Malaya and a general election. There was a picture of Churchill, and George the Fifth. And a photograph of a street in some bombed city, with one-dimensional houses beyond whose glassless windows lay a moonscape of rubble and destruction. She tidied them all on to one shelf, to make some space for John's books, and considered the rest of the room. What had she written in here, great-grandmother? Thank-you letters, invitations, replies to invitations? In the back of a bureau with spindly legs that wavered under pressure, unlike the aunts' sturdy, masculine desks in the study, Clare found yellowing cards, printed with flowing italic script. Professor and Mrs Mayfield had been At Home to their friends on November 15th 1911, at eight o'clock in the evening. A Buffet Supper had been served, and there had been Music. Poor great-grandfather—he would have been more at home on the Fly River, battling with the mosquitoes. And here was a bundle of great-grandmother's housekeeping bills, meticulously checked and annotated (how cheap everything had been—a whole month's groceries, for goodness knows how many people, only ten pounds odd). And a long list of names, Dr and Mrs This, Professor That, the Miss Thoses—what did great-grandmother have in mind for them? Christmas cards, tea, supper, lunch? And here were more yellow cards, on which—goodness!—Mrs Mayfield requested the pleasure of the company of Blank on June 9th 1912 at a Dance in honour of her daughters Susan and Anne. The aunts! Dancing! Had they enjoyed themselves? What had they worn? Clare made a mental note to find out about that, and tidied the contents of the desk away. The desk itself, with silent apologies to great-grandmother, she removed to another room. It was far too flimsy for John, who could have the nice solid table from the sewing-room. The wallpaper was unsuitable—an elaborate affair of tiny blue roses intertwined with other flowers and miles of realistic blue satin ribbon—but nothing could be done about that, nor the curtains, which were of the same inclination. John, used to migrating from room to room, probably wouldn't notice. But how would he get on with great-grandmother—with her remote presence, almost extinguished by time, but surely still faintly clinging to this room, her thoughts, her feelings, her opinions, flickering out from 1911? There could hardly be two people further removed from one another. How odd, how very odd, that the same room should, eventually, have held them both: great-grandmother, in silk and whalebone, her mind furnished in the nineteenth century; John, in jeans and sweater, born thousands of miles away, speaking another language.

Maureen said, 'I don't mind sharing the toilet with him. I mean, I just wanted to make that plain, in case you were thinking I was that type. It doesn't bother me. Not at all.'

Clare saved the matter of the Dance until the weekend, when Aunt Anne, whose cold had been improving steadily all week, got dressed and came downstairs. Mrs Hedges had made a cake in celebration, and Clare, in a fit of ambition, had iced it, and adorned it with glacé cherries. The icing, too thin, had lurched down the sides, carrying most of the cherries with it, but the aunts were much impressed. They had never known how to do things like that.

'How clever,' said Aunt Anne. 'Does it take long to cook?'

'You don't cook it. You mix it up and slosh it on. Most of that sloshed off again.'

The aunts peered. 'The cherries remind me of that hat of mother's,' said Aunt Susan. 'I remember sitting behind it in church, with my mouth watering unbearably. It was like a still-life of fruit salad.'

'I remember,' said Aunt Anne. 'But it had roses, too. You couldn't have eaten the roses.'

'I don't see why not. After all, violets are eaten, when crystallised. I should think certain roses would be delicious. The old-fashioned, scented ones.'

'Not "Peace", or "Queen Elizabeth"—they would be hideously tough.'

'You may be right. Fit only for soup, perhaps.'

Really, the aunts were getting quite out of hand. Clare calmed them down with cups of tea and then said casually, 'Did you enjoy yourselves on June 9th? June 9th 1912?'

They were satisfactorily astonished. And bewildered.

'I have no idea,' said Aunt Susan. 'What were we doing?'

'Dancing.'

'Dancing! Surely not!'

'I know!' said Aunt Anne. 'The dance mother gave for us. You were nineteen and I was seventeen. But how could she know about that!'

'I get these vibrations,' said Clare. "I close my eyes and think myself backwards. Back and back into the past. It's like drowning only nicer. And then I know anything I want to. You have to be frightfully sensitive, of course.'

'Naturally,' said Aunt Susan. 'Only a mind of the greatest refinement ...'

'She has been at that bureau of mother's. There are old invitations in there.'

'What a pity,' said Aunt Susan. 'I was enjoying the stream-of-consciousness idea.'

Clare gave Aunt Anne a look of reproach. 'Anyway, did you?'

'No,' said Aunt Susan. 'To be frank. My dress was too tight, I remember, and I had to dance with the college Chaplain, who was immensely fat, and the Bursar, who trod on my feet and talked endlessly of his mother-in-law.'

Clare said, 'Bother.'

'Why?'

'I thought it would have been like women's magazines. You whirling round and round in the moonlight in his strong arms, his breath warm on your cheek.'

'Absolutely not,' said Aunt Susan. 'It was in the college dining-hall, which is rather harshly lit.'

'I quite enjoyed it,' said Aunt Anne. 'I had my hair up for the first time, and felt extremely mature.'

'Of course it was mother's first attempt to marry us off. Suitable young men had been summoned.'

'Poor mother.'

'It was her one defeat.'

The aunts chuckled. There was a whiff of ancient rebellion in the sober atmosphere of the library.

'Did they propose?' said Clare. 'The suitable young men?'

'Have you no sense of delicacy?' said Aunt Susan severely.

'Sorry. I say, are you going to give a dance for me? When I'm mature?'

'I hadn't realised the tradition persisted. But of course we will.'

'Outside the back door, I think,' said Clare. 'We can move the dustbins. People can overflow into the garden. We'll floodlight it from the kitchen window. The gramophone with the loudspeaker from the attic will do for music. Do you think it would be all right if I wore great-grandmother's red silk dress?'

'I can think of no better use for it,' said Aunt Anne.

'And my hair up. If we can get it there.'

'We will persevere until we do.'

We won't really, Clare thought. But it's a nice joke. I like jokes with the aunts. She lay close to the fire, her face burning, and stared into it: incandescent interiors, gushing flame, logs grey-plated with ash, roaming shadows. I like fires. I like being here, just now, just at this moment. This is one of the times I wouldn't mind stopping at, for ever, or for longer, anyway, if you could kind of freeze yourself. But you can't. It's like being on a train, and seeing a lovely quiet country station with flowers and cows in long grass, and not being able to get off at it.

Thinking of this, she was seized with a feeling of panic, as though everything were slipping from her—the fire, the room, the aunts—and there was no way she could hold any of it. She rolled on her back and stared at the ceiling, overwhelmed with sudden desolation.

Aunt Susan looked down over the top of *The Times* and said, 'I think we should tell Anne what we have done.'

'What? Oh, yes, we should.'

Aunt Anne said, 'Let me guess. There has been a domestic disaster. You have broken mother's Crown Derby tea-set.'

'No. On the contrary, we have done something constructive. We have asked a young African student to come and live here. You will like him. He has the most interesting things to say about the problems of emergent societies.'

Aunt Anne's surprise and faint misgivings turned, with only

a little persuasion, to interest and anticipation.

'We shall be quite a household,' said Aunt Susan. 'I hope he will get on with—what is she called?—Maureen.'

Sunday came, and John with it, his possessions slung around a bicycle in paper bags and parcels tied with string. The bicycle joined Clare's in the shed at the side, and the house absorbed him, as it had absorbed so many other people. Another set of thoughts, and experiences, and attitudes had joined all the others whose misty imprint surely still lingered somehow behind the yellow brick and gothic windows. Yearnings of late Victorian housemaids, boredom of the aunts, cloistered in the schoolroom, the despondency of governesses ... Great-grandmother's busy pursuit of an appropriate and well-ordered life, the heady breeze of the aunts' resolution to determine their own futures ... Friends, relations, students ... And, faintest of all, the alien flavour of remote, half-understood things known only to great-grandmother. The shadows of another world and another time.

CHAPTER 8_____

The ancestors do not come again to the village. Time passes: much time. The old men of the tribe die. Babies are born, and grow up. The boys become men, and the girls women. The tribe are alone, with the yams and the sugar-cane and the pigs, and the cocka-toos in the forest trees, and the blue and scarlet birds of paradise.

'I suppose he'd be well thought of, in his own country?' said Maureen.

'I s'pose so.'

'I mean, when he goes back, he'll be one of the high-ups?'

'He'll be a professor, one day, Aunt Susan says.'

'That's what I thought,' said Maureen. Her face was set in a hard scowl, as though she was working out an impossibly difficult sum in her head, and getting it wrong. She banged out her cigar-ette, and lit another. 'Well, I'd better be off. Time and tide wait for no man. Be seeing you.'

Something had happened to Maureen. She was dislodged, as it were, from certainty, like a person who has moved suddenly from bright sunshine into twilight, and has to grope a little. Her face had a shrouded look, as though on top of her real expression she had tacked another: a faint, fixed smile. If she and Clare were alone together, everything was as it had been, but when John was present, which he often was, since he was a prodigious eater and found his way frequently to the kitchen, she changed. Her voice pitched itself a tone lower, with the words carefully pronounced and separated, as though prepared in advance. She was like someone ordering things from a shop, over the telephone. She called Clare 'dear', and established traditions, small definitions of how things were done here. Breakfast was at eight-fifteen, the bread (everybody's) was in the bin, the marmalade (hers) was on the dresser, we prefer China tea, the chair with arms is Maureen's. 'Do sit here, John,' she would say, 'this side,' pulling up the other one. Her bosom was hitched just a fraction higher under the new blue sweater, her face more closely powdered. The candle-wick dressing-gown no longer came down to breakfast, nor the hair curlers. Talking to John, her voice took on an edge, a hint, a whisper of graciousness, and then faltered with unease. 'I expect you're in a hurry to get off to your classes. Lectures, I mean to say, that is. Let me pour you some tea—milk and sugar?' Lighting a cigarette, she would check the glowing tip, blow out the match with a delicate puff, turn her head away to exude smoke, and hold the white stick between first and second fingers, the hand drooping a little, finger-nails newly painted. When she left the room, there were ponds of fragrance in the air where she had been—'Tweed' and Boots bath oil.

John said sadly, 'I'm afraid Miss Cooper doesn't like me.'

'No,' said Clare. 'It's that she doesn't know how to arrange you in her mind. You know how librarians put books under History or Poetry or Gardening? She doesn't know where to put you, so she's in a fuss.' Having said that, she was amazed. How do I know that? Maureen's nearly thirty. But it's true.

'You may be right,' said John. 'I've interfered with her social perspectives.'

'I wish you wouldn't use words like that.'

'Sorry. I've upset her cataloguing system.'

'That's better, I suppose.'

'I'm a book about electrical engineering, but written in blank verse.'

'Actually,' said Clare, 'she feels you're probably cleverer than she is, and you're a man, so that puts you in one kind of order, but then you're black, and foreign, so that puts you in another, which gets her all muddled.'

'You are a very odd girl—did you know that?'

'Yes.'

'You don't need to look as though you'd done something wrong. Personally I think people are better if they are odd. Your aunts are odd too. You're rather like them, in fact.'

'Am I?' said Clare, delighted. 'Honestly?'

'Of course. You have the same way of going to the middle of things. Not bothering about pretences.'

'My aunts are thought eccentric. That's what our relations say. Polite word for odd.'

'That is because most people are more comfortable with pretences.'

There was a silence, filled with the clock and the pipes and a car revving in the next-door drive.

'I'm not,' said Clare.

'You're very fond of your aunts, aren't you?'

'You can't pretend things are something different, like Maureen's magazines.'

'How long have you lived with them?'

'Everything bright and shining and easy if you use the right shampoo.'

'Here,' said John, 'I thought we were having a conversation. Me saying something and then you answering and then my turn again. That kind of thing.'

'Like tennis?'

'Exactly.'

'Sorry. I got stuck for a moment.'

'I have to go anyway,' said John. 'Work to do. See you later, maybe.'

'Right you are. It's your serve, next time.'

The production of *Macbeth* at school was nearing fruition. Since it was clearly too cumbersome to present the play at full length Mrs Cramp and those responsible had reduced it to a series of the most vital scenes. Clare had no leading part but appeared at various points as a soldier, attendant, or guest at the banquet.

'Actually,' she said to Liz, 'I'm not just any old guest. I'm Lady Macbeth's mother.'

'But it doesn't say anything about Lady Macbeth's mother.'

'Never mind. It doesn't say she wasn't there, either. And you can act better if you know who you are. You can't be very convincing if you don't even know what your name is, can you?'

The dress rehearsal took place before a rapt audience of the ladies from the kitchens, the caretaker and his wife, and anyone else with nothing better to do. Clare, standing in front of the cloakroom mirror, could hear the distant sounds of murder from the stage.

'That's Liz done for,' said someone. 'Poor old Banquo.'

'Mmn.' Clare stared at her face. She rubbed the make-up stick all over her, grease-paint or whatever it was called, and it glowed like a bad case of sunburn. How old would Lady Macbeth's mother have been? Quite old, anyway. She took a stick of black stuff and etched black lines on her forehead, and two black crescents at the side of her mouth. Then she found a finer, grey stick, and drew in smaller lines around her eyes. Grey powder for the hair. She sprinkled it liberally and contemplated the result. A strange, distorted Clare looked back at her. Me in fifty years' time? No, some mad clown, more like.

'How do I look?'

'A bit weird.'

'Old?'

'Not really. You can still see the proper you underneath. P'haps it'll be better from further off.'

Liz, murdered, came back into the cloakroom and shed her costume, peeling off jerkin, hose and doublet like the shell of a chrysalis, to expose a real Liz in vest and pants beneath.

'Is it going all right?'

'Ghastly ... Honestly, Susan dropped the knife and was hunting all over the floor for it and everyone keeps forgetting their lines. What *have* you done to your face? I say, what's happened to the tube of blood?'

'Don't you like my face? You can see different layers of me now.'

'What? Oh, *there's* the blood—you were standing on it all the time. Here, help me get into the cheesecloth.'

Aunt Susan, regretfully, decided that she had better not come to the play. Aunt Anne was not so well, again, and should not perhaps be left on her own. Both aunts were apologetic and disappointed, on their own behalf and because they felt Clare should have family support. 'It's all right,' said Clare. 'John wants to come.'

She considered inviting Maureen as well, and then decided against it. It was not so much that they did not get on as that John's presence somehow induced in Maureen a state of tension that gradually spread to anyone within range. Indeed, even inanimate objects seemed to be affected. In the airing-cupboard, their possessions confronted one another uneasily, John's socks hanging in a row on the hot-pipe, bright reds and greens and purples blossoming in the dark like some irrepressible tropical growth, while on the other side Maureen's white bra and pale blue pants and limp tights were marshalled beyond the boiler, discreetly gleaming and holding their own in an atmosphere of discord. Clare had arranged the clothes horse as a partition in case violence broke out.

Consequently, it was John alone who represented Norham Gardens at the first night of *Macbeth*. Clare, peering through the central gap of the stage curtains, could see him in the middle of a row of parents, looking detached but by no means discomfited. He observed everything with interest. He too, it had been revealed in the kitchen that morning, had acted in Shakespeare.

'When?' said Clare, pouring tonic into a tablespoon.

'At my first school, in the bush. I was a soldier in *Julius Caesar*. My only line was "Hail Caesar", and then we all cheered. Those of us who could not speak much English cheered in our own language. It was very effective. The production took place in the market square and everyone in the village came.'

'Did they know about Romans, and all that?'

'No,' said John, 'but our English master had a firm belief in culture. Your culture. Anyway, everybody enjoyed it. What is that stuff you are taking?'

'Tonic. It strengthens you.'

'My mother used to give me strengthening medicine when I was young. She bought it in the market at Kampala from an Indian grocer. It said on the bottle that if you took it regularly you would be able to strangle a lion with your bare hands.'

'Did you ever try?'

'I came to England instead,' said John, and laughed.

The audience steamed a little in the warmth of the school building. It must have started snowing again: moisture glistened on people's hair and shoulders. Clare, cycling up from Norham Gardens in the darkness, had seen the glow of light from the city reflected in a heavy, orange-looking sky that seemed oppressively close, lurking somehow just above the tops of houses and trees. There was a feeling of suspense, as though, off-stage, something waited.

And Clare, off-stage in the gym, waited through the incantations of the witches for her first scene. People milled around her. Mrs Cramp rushed to and fro, inspiring an atmosphere of crisis. Someone had lost part of her costume. The curtains kept threatening to stick. Macduff had a nose-bleed. Clare, costumed for the banquet scene, sat on a pile of mats while people came and went—ordinary, familiar faces and shapes oddly translated into the shadow of something else. Not the substance, because in no way were these really Shakespeare characters, or even actors, but the shadow of such a thing faintly cast upon faces seen every day, talking, eating, singing, yawning. Faces distorted by make-up, but perfectly recognisable beneath, familiar voices inexpertly proclaiming thoughts and beliefs that could hardly be more inappropriate to a lot of people aged about fourteen leading uneventful lives in the South Midlands. In rehearsal, it had usually seemed funny. Now, for some reason that Clare could not isolate, it no longer was. It was vaguely sinister, as though the pretence might really distort people in some way, unhinge things, as it were, so that you would no longer be sure what was, and what was not.

'Clare! Come *on*!'

Filing on to the stage, with the audience only dimly visible as motionless shapes in the darkened hall, intensified the feeling. Which was real, us or them? Us, up here, all got up in grease-paint and funny clothes, or them, down there, in winter coats and macs and umbrellas hung on the backs of the school chairs? The stage lights isolated the actors, shouldered the audience aside into darkness, made them the unreal observers.

The guests, seated at the table, murmured among themselves. Clare's neighbour, mouthing nonsense, was not Jennie Sanders, who lived in Eynsham and was good at Art, but a stranger, with lined and painted face. Other faces swam in the glare of the lights, haloed and somehow duplicated by an effect of spotlighting. Voices boomed. Banquo's ghost arrived, sat at the table, and was studiously ignored by the other guests. 'Rhubarb, rhubarb,' said the stranger who was Jennie Sanders.

Clare said conversationally, 'Good heavens! there is Banquo's ghost.' The neutral murmurs around turned to murmurs of reproof. Someone said, whispered, 'Shut up, you idiot, we're not supposed to be able to see her—him.' Above them, Macbeth and Lady Macbeth argued out the same point.

'It would be much more interesting if we did,' said Clare. 'Then there'd really be something to talk about.' Beyond her, in the wings, she could see Mrs Cramp making curious gestures, soothing the air with her hands like a conductor restraining an over-active orchestra. She mouthed something: 'Don't talk so loud,' it looked like. Jennie Sanders, under her paint, was registering alarm. 'Or perhaps they did,' said Clare thoughtfully. 'Perhaps that's the whole point. They all saw it, Lady Macbeth specially, but they pretended not to so Macbeth would get in a proper old state.' Around her, the guests were gabbling feverishly. Macbeth raved at the ghost and the ghost got up and left the stage while the guests politely looked the other way. It loitered in the wings, stripping off cheesecloth and becoming Liz again. A disastrous dinner party drew to a close. The guests filed off the stage.

Behind the scenes, Clare was accused by some of frivolity and others of treachery. She hardly heard them: their painted faces, saying things, floated around her. Mrs Cramp appeared and said, 'You were a very convincing guest, I must say, Clare. A bit over-convincing, maybe, but never mind,' and then, 'Are you feeling all right?'

Clare said, 'Can I go home? Would it matter if I didn't come on in the last scene?'

'Of course you can go, if you're not feeling well.'

'I'm all right.'

It was snowing hard. She could hardly see where she went, standing up on the pedals of the bike and pushing forward into the whirling darkness. When she got to Norham Gardens she threw the bike down on the gravel anyhow and left it, wheels still spinning, running up the steps and into the house. She went straight upstairs to the attic, bumping into Maureen who was coming out of the bathroom with a towel wound turban-wise round her head. The kwoi, or tamburan, or shield was where it should be, propped up staring out of the window, and the window was shut, and outside the window it was snowing and through the snow there was a noise, men shouting, far away, and it seemed odd no one else could hear it, only her. She picked up the shield and went downstairs again, past Maureen, who seemed to be saying something, and into the kitchen. She opened the back door and put the shield outside, and then she closed the door, and locked it, and switched out the kitchen lights, and went upstairs to bed.

In bed, hours later, or maybe minutes, she heard footsteps on the stairs, down, and up, and down again. Maureen and John talking. Then someone knocking at the door.

'Come in.'

Maureen had a tray in her hand, with a jug that steamed, and a cup and saucer.

'I've done you a hot drink. Ovaltine.'

'Thanks very much.'

'A lady rang from the school. One of the teachers. She was a bit worried. She said she thought you weren't feeling well. And John missed you somehow. He came home on his own.'

'I'm afraid I forgot about him,' said Clare. 'Please could you tell him I'm sorry.'

Maureen sat down on the end of the bed. 'Yes. He was worried too. He's a nice boy, I'll say that.' She looked at Clare. 'Do you think you're running a temperature?'

'No. It isn't anything like that.'

'Nerves,' said Maureen. 'You get nerves, at your age. My mum says I used to carry on like nobody's business. I don't remember, personally.'

Clare drank. She said, 'I'm a nuisance, aren't I?'

'You can get that idea out of your head for a start,' said Maureen. She fussed round the room for a moment, straightening the curtains, tucking in an end of blanket.

'Think you'll be all right now?'

'Yes. Thank you, Maureen.'

'The teacher said she thought you ought to stop in tomorrow. Not bother with school. Have a bit of a rest.'

'Oh, did she?'

She must have slept very late, because when she woke both Maureen and John had left the house and there was a bright, hard light through the curtains. It would have been too late for school anyway. Presently there were sounds of the aunts getting up, and then the front door banging as Mrs Hedges arrived. After a few minutes she came upstairs, with a piece of paper in her hand.

'Your Maureen left me a note. Thoughtful, that was. You've not been well, she says.'

'It wasn't anything. I just felt a bit odd at the school play and decided not to stay to the end.'

Mrs Hedges drew the curtains. Then she studied Clare. Lying in bed, just woken up, unbrushed and unwashed, it is not possible to create an impression of great health or vigour. 'You look off-colour,' said Mrs Hedges. 'I've seen this coming. A good check-up, that's what you need. I'm ringing the doctor. You can pop along to the surgery this morning.'

'No,' said Clare feebly.

'Yes,' said Mrs Hedges.

'What is it of me that needs checking?'

'Blood pressure and that, I should think.'

'Oh,' said Clare. 'I see.'

'You get yourself dressed, and I'll do you some breakfast. And put something warm on, it's freezing out. By the way, one thing I can't understand—that wood thing from the attic, I found it outside the back door.'

'I put it there,' said Clare.

'Threw it away?'

'Not exactly.'

'Well, I've put it back upstairs. You can't go throwing out things without asking the old ladies. You never know with things, in this house—it might be valuable.'

The doctor, behind his desk, studied a brown card, that, Clare could see, said she had been born on September 11th 1959, had been vaccinated and injected against this and that, had sprained an ankle, had a boil on her leg, two styes, measles, and chicken pox.

'What's the problem?' he said. 'There's a message that you've been a bit off-colour.'

Clare thought. Finally she said, 'I don't sleep very well at night.'

'Ah,' said the doctor. 'Headaches?'

'No headaches.'

'Bowels all right?'

'Fine.'

'Waterworks?'

'Fine too.'

'Everything all right at school?'

'Everything's all right at school.'

'No problems, then?'

'Not really.'

'But you've been feeling off-colour.'

Your doctor is a busy man. Do not waste your doctor's time.

'Sometimes I think I hear things,' said Clare. 'When other people don't.'

The doctor came out from behind his desk. Something cold and shiny was produced through which he peered into Clare's ears, first one, then the other. Clare held back her head, helpfully. 'No infection there,' said the doctor.

He put the steel thing away. 'Anything else?'

'Sometimes things look funny. Striped, when they're not.'

A torch was whipped from the doctor's pocket. 'Head back, please. Ever had an eye test?'

'Last year.'

The torch shone dazzling in the corner of Clare's eye. Beyond it she could see the doctor's face in intimate close-up, every line enlarged, blown-up, one eye squinting at her, gazing down into her eye. And what was he seeing? Her soul, perhaps. A little, soft, wriggling thing deep in the middle of her.

'All in order there,' said the doctor, putting the torch away.

'Oh,' said Clare. 'Good.'

The doctor returned to his desk. He read the brown card through again, while Clare observed that he wore a tie with small cars on it. Old cars with no tops. So the doctor was interested in vintage cars. Now I know more about him than he knows about me. Fifteen love to me.

'Hmm,' said the doctor. 'Yes. Well now—er, Clare—I can't find anything much wrong with you. I think this not sleeping thing will pass off, you know. I expect you've been getting a bit bothered about exams or something, eh? I don't like giving sleeping pills to people of your age. Have a hot drink before you go to bed, and try to relax, see. Read a book—you know, something light, that kind of thing. Unwind.'

'Yes,' said Clare. 'I see. Thank you very much.'

'Splendid,' said the doctor. He tapped the bell on his desk. They smiled over each other's shoulders.

'Goodbye,' said Clare.

'Goodbye,' said the doctor.

'Well?' said Mrs Hedges.

'I'm all in order. Splendid, I am.'

Mrs Hedges whipped a pile of dust into the dustpan and stood up. 'He gave you a proper going-over, did he?' she said suspiciously.

'Ears, eyes, everything. Mrs Hedges ...'

'Yes?'

'Don't tell the aunts I went to the doctor.'

'You don't want them getting bothered?'

'Mmn.'

'You're a good girl,' said Mrs Hedges, 'one way and another. Feeling all right in yourself now, are you?'

'Perfectly. I don't think I'll go to school, though.'

'That's right,' said Mrs Hedges. 'You take it easy. They put too much on you these days, if you ask me, at your age.'

She walked down into the town. The pavements were crunchy with ice, the sky high and white all over, the trees skeletal, mere outlines of themselves. It was as though nature and growth—the world of blue skies and unfurling leaves—had retreated for ever, leaving things to brick, stone and concrete. She wandered through the streets, her cold hands stuck in her pockets, and stared into shop windows. In one, plaster dummies leaped and postured and an artificial sun beamed upon artificial daisies: Get the Young Look for Spring, ordered a banner, draped between the sun and the daisies. In another, strings of paper snowflakes danced above the heads of a smiling, symmetrical family—father, mother, boy and girl—'Beat the Freeze' said the father, 'Go electric!' Advice and instruction battered her from windows and hoardings. Compare our Prices: Go Electric: Shop at the Co-op. A bus stood throbbing at the traffic lights: orange letters at its rear urged her to Hop on a Bus.

Unwind. Take a day off. Hop on a bus.

The bus station was Siberia, swept by freezing winds funnelled from the north. Cigarette cartons spun in the gutters: newspapers flapped like desolate birds. But the destinations on the buses held out a promise of other things—of some distant, indestructible rural summer. Birds, grass, flowers. Chipping Norton, Burford, Stow-on-the-Wold. Clare selected Burford, because she remembered hearing the aunts speak of it, and climbed on to a bus occupied by women with shopping baskets, and a few small children. Presently a driver came, the bus quivered into life, moved out of Oxford along grey streets.

It snows more heavily outside cities. Beyond the houses the fields were ranged one beyond another in pure, receding squares of white. Snow was piled against the dark hedges, too, untrodden and unfouled. From the top of the bus Clare looked down upon small grey villages huddled around church spires. Landscape curved around her in a huge circle, hillsides delicately crested with trees, rivers looping between the blunt winter shapes of willows, white fields furrowed with brown where snow had melted on the plough. The horizons seemed huge, reaching away into unseen white distances, as though England were some great continent, the bus and its passengers moving ant-like through it. And then the scale would be reversed as they came into a village and the bus towered above cottages and Clare, through a shield of steamy glass, looked down into windows that presented the blank wooden backs of dressing-tables. They followed the rim of a shallow valley where a river wound through flat fields, shining, and small golden stone buildings shouldered out from hedges and hillsides. They swung round a corner, the bunchy women gathered themselves and stood rocking as the bus came to a stop. Everyone got off.

The shops in Burford gave neither instruction or advice. They had discreet and neutral windows beyond which lurked single, old, expensive pieces of furniture. Although people walked the pavements, there was a feeling of desertion as though this were a place from which, a long time ago, everyone had gone. The rows of parked cars glittered strangely in the wide street that seemed to descend straight into a bowl of fields and hills, neatly punctuated by the church spire at the bottom. Every building was old, many were beautiful: they seemed to be there together in sad abandonment like textbook illustrations of the past. Clare bought a bun from a warm stuffy shop that consoled with its notices about Typhoo Tea and Green Shield stamps. She walked down towards the church, eating.

The names began in the churchyard, cut deep into tombstones

and elaborately carven memorials behind rusting iron railings. She wandered among them, reading of Eliza Matthews, of This Parish, Dearly Loved, who Departed this Life on July 7th, 1786, of Thomas James Hammond, Husband and Father, and Jane Parsloe, Infant Daughter. She went into the church and names clustered on every wall, a precise, enduring, stone record of the people who had lived in this place. Here were insistent memories, the determination of people that they should not be forgotten, and the determination of others not to forget, the whole matter carefully reduced to the scoring of elaborate script upon stone, marble, lead and brass.

Clare, her hands in the pockets of her school coat, her face stinging from the cold, moved slowly round the church, staring at one inscription after another, giving her attention to the whole chronicle of wood merchants, burghers and benefactors of the poor, of husbands and fathers, wives, mothers and children. She felt an obligation to listen. It would be nice, she thought, to be a person living in this place and sit every Sunday beside these names, especially if maybe they were the same as your own name, or people you knew. You would feel settled, if you were a person who did that. She stood in front of a marble slab shaped like a shield that told her of Susan Mary Partredge, A Loving and Dutiful Daughter, Devoted Mother and Beloved Wife, and thought it curious that two different lots of people so very far removed from each other should wish to preserve their feelings about what had gone before in such a similar way. Only here they put it into words, not shapes and patterns and colours.

She went out into the churchyard, through the silence and into the street again. She stood by herself at the bus stop, and waited to go home.

CHAPTER 9

*In other parts of the island, the motor-car has arrived,
and the tractor. Houses are built, and roads con-
structed. A war is fought, with aeroplanes and guns.
There are new things on the island now: money and
Coca-Cola, and Lucky Strike cigarettes, and paraffin
and rifles and penicillin. The tribe know nothing of
this. Sometimes they see and hear things that are
strange, but they have always known the world to be
an uneasy and unpredictable place, so they placate
the spirits and plant their yams at the proper time.*

'I'm sorry about last night,' said Clare. 'Leaving you at the school
like that.'

John was in his room—great-grandmother's writing-room—sitting
at the desk. Books were ranged around him in untidy heaps.
'Don't worry,' he said. 'Are you feeling better now?'

'Yes, thank you. What did you think of the play?'

'It was interesting,' said John politely. 'I liked the ghost.'

'She's my best friend. Liz.'

'Please give her my congratulations.'

Clare sat on the bed. There was a photograph of John's parents,
framed, on the bedside table, and another of a whole row of
brothers and sisters, diminishing in size from a tall schoolboy in
shorts with long legs and bony knees to a plump and broadly
smiling baby. She said, 'Do you miss them?'

'Yes. Very much.'

'Your clock's wrong.'

'No. It is set the same as Kampala time.'

'So that it doesn't feel so far away?'

'That's right,' said John. 'What have you been doing today? I hear you had a day off from school.'

'First I went to see the doctor and he looked inside me and said I was all in order. And then I took a bus into the country and read the names on the walls of a church.'

'I visited Westminster Abbey last year. There are a great many names there. Famous names.'

'These weren't famous,' said Clare. 'Just names. I'd better go and get the supper with Aunt Susan.'

'So ...' said Aunt Susan. 'How did the play go? I quite forgot to ask.'

'All right. They were rather cross with me. I started talking in the banquet scene.'

'Surely you were supposed to? As a guest.'

'I said I could see Banquo's ghost. You aren't supposed to do that.'

Aunt Susan let her glasses slide to the end of her nose and looked over the top of them: a sharp, querying look. 'Why?'

'I don't know really. I was feeling a bit peculiar. I expect it's the weather.'

'Nonsense. Only the very weak in spirit allow themselves to be directed by weather. Is there something on your mind?'

'No.'

'Perhaps you need a change. Why don't you do something interesting at the weekend? Go somewhere with a friend.'

'Liz has got her grandmother coming to stay.'

'Someone else, then. Go to London for the day.'

'London?' Trains, traffic, shops, Piccadilly Circus, Buckingham Palace, all that ...

'Why not? See if your friend John would like to escort you. Show him the sights.'

During the day, working mechanically through the things that had to be done—go to school, go here, go there, do maths, Latin, history, eat, run about—the idea bloomed a little in her mind and became attractive. An outing. An occasion. She hoped John would like the idea, not have engagements, or, even, not wish to do something with her. She wrote in her otherwise empty diary (a Christmas present from Norfolk, labelled 'From the children, with love', in cousin Margaret's writing)—'To London', and underlined it neatly. The day rolled on, and away: she felt lethargic, glad to have the dictation of the school day around her which removed any obligation to make decisions, think what to do next. It was a relief to obey bells, and the clock. Nobody mentioned her misdemeanour at the play: like the play itself, it had vanished into the past and no longer mattered particularly. Mrs Cramp asked if she was feeling better, and hoped she had rested at home yesterday. Yes, said Clare, I rested at home yesterday, and I am quite all right now.

Once, the chronology of the day failed altogether. Sitting at her desk, waiting for whatever came next, she could not remember whereabouts they might be. She said to Liz, 'Is it morning or afternoon?'

'Morning, silly. Half past eleven.'

She had, for a moment, felt suspended in time. Untethered. Everything had been as usual—the formroom, the blackboard, the games pitch framed in the window—but she herself had seemed to be unrelated to everything else. To know that it was half past eleven was to lurch, with relief, into place again.

'Have you ever done that? Not known what time of day it was?'

Liz considered. 'Not lately. I used to when I was small. I remember rushing to my mother to find out if it was before lunch or after.'

'Why do you think it matters so much?'

'I don't know. It's just unsettling, somehow. You don't know where you are.'

With some diffidence—was she being impertinent, perhaps?—she put the suggestion about London to John that evening. To her relief, he thought it a good idea.

'Where shall we go?'

'I don't know,' said Clare. 'What have you seen in London?'

'The Houses of Parliament. Oxford Street. Paddington Station.

Big Ben. Trafalgar Square. The Ugandan High Commissioner's office.'

'And Westminster Abbey.'

'Yes. Westminster Abbey.'

'We could go to the Zoo,' said Clare. 'If it's cold they have nice stuffy places there. The Lion House, and that kind of thing.'

'Are you trying to make me feel at home?' said John gravely. They both laughed.

It did not snow again that week, but it became no warmer. The old snow lay around in dirty heaps, tinged grey or brown. In the garden it had flattened into a skin of ice over the grass, and the grass pricked through it here and there, looking artificial. Clare, listening to weather forecasts with an interest beyond the immediate present, heard that milder weather was expected over the weekend, and was pleased. They would not have to spend all their time in the Lion House.

There were white skies on Saturday, but no wind, and no snow. They had an early breakfast, supervised by Maureen, who was faintly disapproving. Clare, filled suddenly with compunction, thought perhaps she should have been asked to come as well, and asked if she would like to. But Maureen was going to help her friend look at material for wedding-dresses. Only the under-occupied, she implied, could be involved in such frivolities as day-trips to London.

The station was bleak, an unpromising starting-point. Bleak with newness, rather than the expected squalor of stations. Tickets were bought from a man so quarantined behind glass that even money and tickets were swivelled on a metal plate rather than passed from hand to hand. It would be dreadful, Clare thought, to start some huge, important journey from here. Travel could never seem momentous under such circumstances—it reduced everything to the stature of a day-trip. As they stood waiting she thought of trains in old films, oozing steam, lumbering slowly away, so that the heroine's face could vanish gradually, irrevocably, into white clouds. You couldn't have a tragic farewell with brisk, matter-of-fact trains of today, whisking commuters and day-trippers through tidy landscapes. She thought of John, leaving home for three years.

'How did you come here?'

'By 'plane.'

Undramatic, too, surely? 'Did all your family come to see you off?'

'Thirty-seven people.'

'Heavens! Was there a lot of crying?'

'Naturally,' said John, with pride.

The Thames valley unrolled on each side of them, trim with whitened fields and black hedges. The back gardens of houses ran down to the railway, offering the traveller a view, that seemed intrusive, of other people's domesticity—washing on lines, children's toys, plaster gnomes, greenhouses. The houses became closer together, the gardens diminished, and were no longer there. The train arrived at Paddington.

'I think,' said John, as though he had given the matter much serious consideration, 'you should show me something very old. Something to do with English history.'

Clare thought, and suggested the Tower. They studied the map of the underground, argued about routes, and found that Clare was more efficient in this area than John, This, for some reason, entertained John vastly. They travelled to the Tower laughing, so that people stared at them, and looked away in embarrassment.

They walked by the river, in a grey pearly light, with a cold wind coming at them from the water, channelled up from Southend, Foulness, the open sea. The city blinked and snapped around them, light answering light, window to window, car to car. The flat slabs of new office blocks, factories, flats, rose among spires and domes. Clare tried to remember fragments of text-book history for John—the Romans, Wat Tyler, the Great Fire—confused herself and him and started them off laughing again. They leaned over a wall and watched the river run brown below them, lining its shore with a scum of oil and rubbish. John found the Tower smaller than he had expected. Inside, he bought a guide book and insisted on establishing their precise whereabouts at every step.

'Wait. We have to go next to the Bloody Tower, or I shall lose my way on the map.'

Clare, preferring to wander undirected, found herself alone from time to time, and would come upon him as though upon a stranger, a long, gawky figure in a leather jacket, studying suits of armour with the intensity of someone who might be required to answer questions on the subject.

They finished the Tower, and emerged at the other end. 'Now where?' said John. 'The lions?'

They made their way to the Zoo deviously, with many changes of route, swaying on the tops of buses, plunging into the hot gale of the Underground, walking. They ate hamburgers in a warm steamy café, and talked. About John's brothers and sisters, about the moon, currently being re-visited by the Americans, about the aunts, about hamburgers, and whether they are best fat or thin, with or without onion. Fed, and warmed, they found themselves another bus, and travelled to the Zoo, to what seemed an elegant fringe of the City, green with grass and trees, the houses huge, trim and withdrawn.

The Zoo, at first, appeared to have been abandoned, by animals, at any rate. People drifted across wastes of grey tarmac, staring hopefully into empty cages, or at inert heaps of fur or feathers bundled away under straw. Pigeons and sparrows gobbled the offerings of small children. From time to time jungly shrieks rang out across the flowerbeds and wire-netting.

'Do *all* animals hibernate over here?' said John.

The monkey house, warm and stinking, was more active. They moved slowly past the cages, reading names and countries of origin. The monkeys swarmed, screamed, stared with sharp, unfathomable eyes. A group of middle-aged women stood in front of the orang-utans and shrieked with laughter. They became almost hysterical, tears rolling down their cheeks. The orang, hunched against the bars, looked immeasurably ancient, a pile of wrinkles from which glittered black, watching eyes.

Clare said, 'Why do animals make people laugh?'

'Perhaps they aren't really laughing. In Uganda people sometimes laugh at road accidents.'

'Do wild animals look different?'

'Smaller,' said John.

They left the monkeys and went to look down into a concrete pit. A brown bear, like a shambling mat edged with claws, wandered up and down, sniffing at empty crisp packets and iced lolly sticks. Clare said suddenly, 'I've seen that before.'

'That bear, particularly?'

'One like it, anyway. Seeing it made me remember—I must have been here with my parents, when I was very young. I can remember not being high enough to see over the railings, and someone lifting me.'

'Was that long before they died?'

The bear sat down on its haunches, licking its paws. 'You're one of the first people I've heard say that. Just like that. Usually they said, "When your mum and dad—er, ..."'

'I thought you didn't like pretences.'

'I don't. But people mostly do, and I don't know how you stop them. You end up pretending yourself.'

'Do you remember them well?' said John.

'Oh, yes. My mother was rather like Aunt Susan, only much younger, of course. She had the same kind of pointed nose. She used to wear a pink dress I liked very much. My father was very tall—or perhaps it was just me being small then, but I remember always turning upwards to look at him. It's funny, but the part of him I remember best is his trousers. Hairy ones, or grey flannel.'

'Did you go straight away to live with your aunts?'

'No. I was six and I lived for about three years with my mother's sister—Aunt Mary—because she had children too. But then they went away to America and the aunts had been asking for me to come to Norham Gardens for a long time, and I wanted to, so I did. I always liked the aunts best, really.'

The bear, its toilet completed, reared suddenly on to its hind legs, turning its snout up to them.

'You feel you ought to give it something,' said Clare.

'He looks extremely well fed to me. Can we find somewhere warm? This is a very cold place.'

The Reptile House was pleasantly warm—quiet, too, and unsmelly. The snakes, in glass tanks set in the wall and lit from within so that they shone in the darkness, individual glowing cases, slithered in their own silent world, tongues flickering like dry flame, or hung in coils around sculptural branches.

'We have those at home,' said John, pointing. A bright, patterned snake lay against the glass, basking in the sun of a sixty-watt bulb.

They moved to the next tank. 'Chameleon,' Clare read, 'Northern Africa and the Middle East.' The chameleon was at the top of a small dead tree, motionless, holding up a limb that ended in a two-fingered foot, like some heraldic creature frozen in mid-movement. With infinite slowness it placed the foot upon a twig, inched forward, hauled up another leg. It seemed, behind its glass, to be living at a different rate, another dimension of time, its hands and feet clenching and unclenching with slow deliberation, its eye swivelling to observe the twig, the floor, the watchers. Did people, to it, seem like the background of a speeded-up film, dashing hither and thither in a frenetic state of near collision? Clare, leaning forward to examine it more closely, saw that its eyes, in fact, swivelled independently so that it stared at the same moment up and down, in front and behind. Its world must be a globe, a bubble of light and colour where nothing was concealed, where there were no beginnings and no ends, no before and no after. It seemed, like the orang, to be of great antiquity, crouched there on its twig with tilted profile and tail curled in a delicate spiral; antique, bloodless, and quite remote.

'You seem very fond of this creature,' said John.

'Not really. It's just the odd way it can see in all directions at once.'

'Must be interesting.'

'No,' said Clare. 'Awful. Let's go.'

The elephants, by comparison, were endearing. They were inside, well away from the cold in a building that displayed them like actors in a lavish production. They swayed and shuffled against backgrounds as cunningly lit and structured as a stage-set. Even so, it was possible to establish some kind of relationship with them: their trunks groped towards the audience as though seeking not food but reassurance of some kind. Here, people gazed more than they laughed.

'I like elephants,' said Clare.

'Most people do.'

'They look a million years old, too.'

'No,' said John, reading a label. ' "Samantha, female African elephant, born at London Zoo 20.1.61".'

'So she's never even been to Africa.'

'No. She's an immigrant, born here.'

'Goodbye, Samantha,' said Clare. 'We've got to catch our train.'

It was twilight when they got to Paddington, and night when they reached Oxford again, black winter night spiked with the flat light from street lamps, shop windows and cars. The train had rushed them through a darkness so dense that, pressed up against the window with no prick of light to define distance, it might have ended a yard or two away, or reached back beyond the train for ever. Travelling in space must be like that, Clare had said to John, and this had led on to other things. How people could ever have thought the world was flat. How they could ever have arrived at the idea of infinity. ('It's frightening,' said Clare, 'it's the most frightening thing in the world. Beyond the world, I mean. There, that's why.') What they thought the sky was.

'It would be much more obvious,' said Clare, 'to think of it as solid. A kind of upside-down bowl. And the sun moving. Like the Greeks thinking it drove across the sky in a chariot.'

'There are tribes in South America who believe you can catch the sun in a net. Or that you must re-light it with burning arrows after an eclipse.'

'Like whistling for a wind.'

'Primitive tribes,' said John, 'can't bear the idea that things are uncontrollable. Fate and time and disaster. Magic has to counteract magic.'

'But it doesn't. You can't ever stop things happening if they're going to.'

'Ah,' said John, '*you* know that. People have been telling you about history for years.'

'Does being told about history help?'

'Knowing about time does. Being able to remember.'

Back at Norham Gardens, they drank hot soup in the kitchen,

and thanked each other for the day. It had, Clare thought, been one of the best days for ages, but now that it was over she felt tired, and a silence had grown up between them. John read the newspaper, frowning at something, withdrawn into a world of other, adult, preoccupations. Clare thought of homework she had not done. Presently they said goodnight and parted.

Clare went to see the aunts in the library.

'Well—there you are! Did you have a good journey?' said Aunt Susan. 'On these nice clean new trains?'

'Didn't you like steam trains?' said Clare, with an obscure sense of disappointment.

'Not particularly. Smuts got in your eyes, and dirt permeated everything. One's clothes were filthy by the end of a journey. I hear Oxford station is much improved, too.'

'They keep the people who sell tickets behind glass, like snakes in the Reptile House.'

'Indeed?' said Aunt Susan. 'I should rather like to see that. And did you enjoy yourselves?'

'Yes, thank you. It was a lovely day.'

In bed, she turned the light off and left the curtains open. She had always liked to watch the light from passing cars roam across the walls and ceiling. There was a vague satisfaction in listening for the hustle of tyres on the road, the swelling whisper of sound, and predicting the exact moment at which the yellow beam would slide through the window, creep up and across, and vanish again. She lay, half asleep, and saw it happen, once, twice. The third time it was not the headlights of a car at all, but sunshine. The sunshine gradually filled the room and she knew that somehow the winter must have passed, without her realising it, and spring have come, or even summer. She got up and dressed, putting on some clothes that were lying across the end of the bed. They must, she thought, have belonged to one of the aunts, because as soon as she had them on, and examined herself in the mirror, she realised that she looked very like the photograph in the drawing-room, where they stood together on a lawn. There was a blouse with a high tight neck and elaborate sleeves ending in neat buttoning at the wrist, a full, heavy skirt, clamped firmly at the waist with a heavy belt, and rather uncomfortable shoes. Standing in front of the mirror, she knew that she must put up her hair, and did so, finding to her surprise that it was quite easy, with thick, long hairpins that were lying about on her dressing-table. This done, she went to the window. The street was very quiet and empty except for a cat sprawled in the shadow of the wall opposite. She could hear some children playing in a garden, and from the Parks, the wooden click of a bat hitting a ball. This made her want to be out of doors, in the sunshine, and she went quickly downstairs. The house had a feeling of activity. She saw no one, but there was an impression that behind the closed doors there were people doing things. Going out of the front drive, she looked back and saw a window opened, and a feather duster vigorously shaken. There were clatterings in the kitchen.

She walked along Norham Gardens and round the corner to the Parks. The new buildings in Parks Road had all gone, and in their place were houses like her own. One, indeed, was still being built. Workmen in cloth caps were bricklaying and trundling wheelbarrows along wooden ramps. Walking past them, she said, 'Good morning.' The one nearest her looked up and said, 'Morning, miss.' There were no cars. A milk-cart, drawn by a brown pony, came past Keble and went round the corner into Museum Road, clinking and spraying a cloud of dust from the untarmacked road. Indeed, everything was very dusty—the leaves on the young trees and the newly planted hedges that edged the gardens. The place had a feeling of incompletion, as though it were waiting for things to happen to it, which was strengthened by the noise the workmen were making, and the scaffolding that stuck up beyond the trees in Banbury Road.

The Parks, on the other hand, were drowsy with heat and summer. The long grass brushed her skirt and she would have liked to take off the heavy shoes but for an obscure feeling that to do so would draw attention to herself. There were quite a lot of people about—women wearing clothes like her own, and men in blazers and flannel trousers. Two of these, passing her, smiled briefly and raised their hats to her. Flat, straw hats. Clare, confused, looked away and walked on towards the river. The game of cricket that she had heard from the house was being played on the pitch at the centre of the Parks, watched by a small crowd of people sitting on deck-chairs, or lying about on the grass. As she passed, the batsman hit a four and there was a flutter of applause. A man shouted, 'Well played!'

The river was dappled with sunlight. The willows poured down into it, the water snatched gently at the bank here and there, ducks cruised, upended, and surfaced again, tails twitching. There was a blue haze between the water and the trees, a misty light in which clouds of midges hung motionless, like smoke. A punt, poled by a tall man with drooping moustache, came downstream, carrying two young women who lay on cushions talking and laughing. On the far bank, brown cows grazed in the water-meadows, their tails swishing the meadowsweet and buttercups.

And beyond the cows there was a disturbance of some kind. There were people there, moving to and fro, half-seen behind a line of stunted trees. They were dark shadows at the edge of the green, at the edge of this tranquil world, and Clare, standing on the river bank and staring over the glassy surface of the water, knew that it was her they wanted. And as soon as she knew this, she was filled with a sense of great urgency. She must get to them before it was too late. Before they went, or before they were unable to tell her what was wrong. She looked round for some way to cross the river. The little arched bridge that she remembered was not there, but further along there was a raft-like object, a flat wooden platform with a punt pole laid across it. She jumped on to this, though it lurched disconcertingly, and managed to push it across the river.

As soon as she reached the other side she began to run through the water-meadow, stumbling through the tangles of flowers and long grass, towards the brown people, who were going away all the time, retreating behind the willows and alders. She opened her mouth to call them, but no sound would come. They were watching her and slipping away from tree to tree, bush to bush, and then stopping to crouch down and watch. Once, her foot caught under the edge of something in the grass, and she nearly fell—looking down she saw that the portrait of great-grandfather from the dining-room was lying there, the glass cracked, and wondered who could have been so careless as to leave it out here. She wanted to pick it up, but there was no time. Already the people were slipping away into the next field. And then, all of a sudden, it came to her that what they wanted was the thing from the attic. The shield. She stopped abruptly, angry with herself for having been so stupid. 'Wait!' she called, and this time her voice came out quite clearly, very loud in the quiet field. 'Wait! I'm going to get it. I'll bring it here to you.'

They stopped going away. She could see them, shadowy beyond a brown ridge of docks, and feel them watching her, and she turned and began to run back, across the field, and over the river again on the raft, and through the Parks. It seemed to take no time at all—she was running, breathless, and there was grass, and trees, and then suddenly she was opening the door at Norham Gardens, and going into the hall.

And the shield was lying in the middle of the hall. Smashed in pieces. Splintered, broken. And she began to cry.

CHAPTER 10_____

*The old men and women of the tribe tell stories to
their children and to their grandchildren; stories of
spirits and gods and of how the world began. One
day, they tell them, the ancestors will come to us,
bringing gifts. The tribe listen, and dig their gardens,
and attend to the pigs. In the next valley, there are
bulldozers clearing the forest. A road is being built,
and a mining company is exploring the soil for
minerals. The tribe, who have never climbed the
mountain because there are bad spirits up there, see
and hear nothing.*

'What *are* you doing?' said Maureen. 'Rattling around in that
attic at this hour of the morning.' She stood outside the lavatory
door, yawning, her hair in curlers.

'Nothing. I just wanted to see something was all right.'

'Have a good day yesterday?'

'Great.'

'Brocade, we got in the end. A courtelle mixture with a raised
motif. Eight yards. She's having the train coming right down from
the shoulder yoke.'

'Lovely,' said Clare.

And the portrait was in the dining-room, of course, not in the
long grass of the water-meadows on the other side of the Cherwell.
Clare, standing in front of it, saw for the first time that the title
of the book great-grandfather held open on his knee was decipher-
able—*The Golden Bough: A Study in Magic and Religion.* A

tricky bit of painting, that must have been. It was a very precise portrait, though, each whisker indicated, as much attention devoted to buttonholes and lapels as to eye and nose. Great-grand-mother, on the other hand, had been allowed a certain lack of definition—beyond her, the background disintegrated into swirls of colour, the lace that edged her dress was a drift of smoke.

'Clare!'

'Coming.'

Aunt Anne was feeling better. She had come down to breakfast, which was eaten in the breakfast-room, with the table pulled up close to the gas-fire. The fire made a loud hissing noise, like a stream, or trees in a wind, and the flames were blue, gushing around the columns of grey stuff that became an incandescent red. The toaster, which trapped slices of bread and burned them unless closely supervised, creaked and throbbed. The aunts looked out of the window and told each other it would snow again.

'You're very silent, child. Don't you like the prospect of more snow? It does improve the look of the place, one must admit.'

'No,' said Clare. The aunts looked at her with gentle surprise.

'I hate this winter. I feel as though time had stuck. Last night I dreamed it was summer.'

'One usually does,' said Aunt Anne. 'Odd. Or not so odd, really, I suppose. Like in dreams one is always young.'

'True,' said Aunt Susan. 'A curious piece of self-deception, when you come to think about it. But it is perfectly true, one does.'

Clare said, 'You mean you dream about the past? Yourself in the old days?'

'Not necessarily. The time can be now—one's body has been readjusted, that is all.' Aunt Susan took a piece of toast and put butter and marmalade on it with slow movements.

'I don't,' said Clare. 'I dream I'm older, often. I did last night.'

'And was that interesting?'

'I don't know, really.' She went over to the window and stared out. The aunts were right: it was snowing already. The trees and houses were shuttered off: the air whirled and thickened as she watched.

The house was locked in its own silence all day. The aunts

stayed in the library. Maureen had gone by train to visit her parents. John left after breakfast with some friends, small, bespectacled, courteous men, and was not seen again. Clare roamed up and down the stairs, going into rooms and coming out again, purposelessly. She stood in the drawing-room, staring at the hunched, unused chairs and sofas as though she had never seen them before. Once, Aunt Susan, climbing the stairs, found her standing in front of the grandfather clock.

'What is the matter, my dear? You look quite panic-stricken.'

'It's stopped.'

'So it has. We forgot to wind it.'

'You never have before.'

'Haven't I? Well, it's soon put right. There ...'

And the snow fell. Indiscriminately, blotting out grass and pavements and road alike so that by evening the houses stood in a strange, undefined landscape neither town nor country. Cars were silenced and slowed, creeping past with diffidence, as though perhaps they had no business here. With darkness came a deep silence. Clare, lying in bed, awake in dark reaches of the night, strained for sounds and heard nothing. She could have been deaf, enclosed within her own mind and body. She had to get up and open the window to reassure herself. Somewhere, a car door banged and people shouted to one another. She went back to bed again.

The telephone rang while she was having breakfast alone. Far away, on a line that seemed to fight through gales or under seas, Mrs Hedges' distorted voice was saying that she wouldn't be coming this morning. Something about Headington Hill, and Linda going down with 'flu.

'What?'

The telephone crackled, clicked, and Mrs Hedges wasn't there any more. Clare put the receiver down and went back into the kitchen. She washed her cup and plate, dried them, and put them away. She told the aunts about Mrs Hedges and took the bus to school, walking the last part among children who whooped in the snow and threw snowballs at each other. Their voices seemed unnaturally loud, as though trapped by the cold. She went past them, and into school.

Art. Up in the high, light, glassy Art Room, which, today, reflected the white glow from outside so that to look up from the paper was almost painful, Clare drew intently, hunched over the table. Somewhere outside her Mrs Elliott was talking, striding among the tables, her long, rather dirty skirt brushing from time to time against people's ankles. 'You want to get a sort of *textural* feel,' she was saying, 'if you see what I mean. A sort of depth. You must bring things together in a kind of focus, do you see?' Nobody spoke, or, apparently, listened: pencils scratched on paper, brushes clinked on the sides of jam-jars. Mrs Elliott waved her cigarette in emphasis of texture, or foci, and paused behind a chair. 'Quite nice, Susan. Good planes. I'd like to see a bit more colour contrast.' She moved on and leaned over Clare's shoulder.

'That's rather effective. Couldn't you develop the pattern a little more at the top?'

'No,' said Clare.

'But it's a bit unbalanced, my dear. Look ...' A hand swooped round Clare's back and came down on to the paper, making swift black lines with marker pencil. 'This is just a suggestion ... It's only a sketch so far, isn't it? You can start again.'

'Stop it!' said Clare violently, jerking the paper. The marker pen clattered to the floor. Mrs Elliott made a startled and indignant noise.

'It has to be like this. That's how it is. This is how they made it.'

Liz, leaning over the table, said, 'It's that thing from your attic, isn't it?'

'What thing?' said Mrs Elliott.

'Nothing,' said Clare sullenly. She reached for a clean sheet of paper and began again, filling in the outline. Mrs Elliott said, 'Well, there's no need to be rude,' and went away, smoking energetically. People's heads crouched an inch or two lower over the tables and the brushes clicked in the jars. Outside, the games field was a blinding, uninterrupted white.

Later, during a lesson, English or History or something, she stared out of the window again and was astonished at the tumultuous noise of rooks, circling above the chestnut trees beyond the tennis court. She could not remember ever having noticed them before. Now, they filled the sky, rising and falling, twisting, swirling away all together, returning ... And the noise they made, the persistent harsh crying, was louder than anything else. A sad, timeless noise, drowning everything. The teacher's voice could hardly be heard. Surely she would have to stop? But everyone else was listening to the lesson, leaning back in their chairs, or propped with elbows on the desk. Someone put a hand up: 'Please ...' Clare blinked, and tried to hear above the clamour of the birds.

At dinner-time, people went out into the snow. The games pitch and tennis courts were covered with flying black figures. Everything was black and white: white ground, white sky, black hedges and fences and dark, stripped trees. Sounds were distorted: unnaturally loud, girls' voices, the small aeroplane creeping just above the horizon, or hushed, like the cars that moved slowly up and down the whitened street. Liz talked of plans for a cycling tour in the spring holidays. Youth Hostels in the Cotswolds. Clare could find nothing to say. Spring? This year, next year, sometime, never.

'Don't you want to come?'

'I don't know,' said Clare dully.

Liz said, 'Well, suit yourself,' and walked away, offended.

Coming home, she could see no light in any of the front windows. The house presented a blank and empty face. She ran up the steps and in at the front door, calling, and came face to face with John at the foot of the stairs.

'What's wrong? What's the matter?'

'I thought there was no one here. No lights ...'

'Your aunts are upstairs, I think. Calm down—everything is as usual. How is the snow? More?'

Clare said, 'Yes, I think so—I'm not sure.' John looked at her, puzzled, and went away into the twilight with his head buried in a vast scarf.

She was walking down Norham Gardens but it had become much longer, and wider, more of an avenue than a street, like some continental city—Paris, maybe, or Vienna—and it wasn't level any more, but quite steeply sloping, so that she climbed as she walked.

There were trees set in the pavements at either side, each one tidily circled by a low iron railing, neat trees with oblong leaves and smooth grey trunks. There was no traffic, and no people. No one in sight at all: she was entirely alone in this urban landscape. The houses reached up the hill ahead of her, and the problem was to find her own, because the numbers had disappeared, and they all looked exactly the same.

Or nearly the same—several times she stopped to stare uncertainly at a house which would then betray itself by an unfamiliar fire-escape, or glass conservatory tacked on to one side, or the wrong combination of gothic windows. She moved on, hurrying. Somewhere, the aunts were waiting for her. They would be worried: she was late already. The place was absolutely silent, and the houses seemed lifeless—no curtains at the windows, no lights. She crossed from one pavement to the other, searching. Examining each house, rejecting it, moving on. And at last she reached the right one, nearly at the top of the long hill. It was right, she knew, because of the blistered black paint on the front door and the brass knocker shaped like a dolphin that the aunts brought back from a holiday, a long time ago.

She ran up the steps, and saw suddenly that there was no glass in the windows. No glass, and weeds clawing up through cracks in the steps. She opened the front door, and there was nothing beyond but daylight and a huge expanse of rubble linking all these houses. They were façades, with nothing beyond—the shadow of houses, homes, sheltering nothing but broken bricks and dust.

All week, the snow lay, and fell again, and lay. The newspapers relegated politicians, crime and the economy to inner pages and allowed the weather first place. Statistics were produced: more roads were blocked than ever before, more trains idle, it was the worst winter since 1963, and, before that, 1947.

'Nineteen forty-seven I shall not forget,' said Aunt Anne. 'We got the old pram down from the attic and wheeled it to the coal depot beyond the station.'

'So we did. And one ate the most unlikely food. Whalemeat, and powdered egg.'

'I wasn't born,' said Clare.

'No, indeed, you were a treat to come.'

'A Post War Credit,' said Aunt Susan. 'Butter, please.'

'A what?'

'I was being facetious. Post War Credits were a kind of post-poned financial bonus to compensate people for the deprivations of the war. Shouldn't you be off to school?'

'I s'pose so.'

She had this reluctance, nowadays, to leave the house. Ordinarily, you went out in the morning and, one way and another, you didn't really think about it all the time you were somewhere else. The aunts, maybe, from time to time, in snatches: you knew they were there, and they'd be there in the evening when you got back, and that was all there was to it. Now, she had to drag herself away in the mornings, and during the day, looking out of a window, going up and down stairs, eating in the clatter of the dining-hall, her thoughts would home on Norham Gardens, as though, unless she did so, it had no substance. She had to create it in her mind, the rooms, the things in the rooms. There was somebody the aunts had talked about once, a philosopher or something like that, who said things weren't there unless you could see them. Or, at least, how could you prove they were there ... It was like that with Norham Gardens.

She took to telephoning during the day, for the reassurance of hearing the aunts' voices, or Mrs Hedges. She invented fragile reasons: was there any shopping they wanted done? She just wanted to say she might be a bit late back this afternoon. As soon as she put the receiver down the feeling of uncertainty would come back and she would stand looking at the telephone, wanting to pick it up again. Sitting at her desk, she drew diagrams of the house over and over again on pieces of blotting-paper, or in exercise books—front elevation, rear elevation, cross-sections with the front removed, like a dolls' house, plans of each room, like an architect's blueprint. She spent long minutes on the exact arrangement of pieces of furniture and pictures, angry and frustrated when she could not remember exactly how everything went. She could not pay attention to other things, and did not do her work properly.

Exercise books came back to her with long comments in red ink—irritated or puzzled. She pushed them into her desk without reading them.

Once, telephoning at mid-day, she found herself speaking to Maureen, returned during her lunch-hour to cook herself baked beans in the kitchen. Confused, Clare asked if everything was all right. Maureen's voice, somehow at the same moment both down at the other end of North Oxford and here, in the voice-piece of the telephone, an inch or two from Clare's chin, said that of course everything was all right and what's up with you. 'Nothing,' said Clare. 'Nothing, really.' Later, that evening, or the next, Maureen remembered.

'What were you on about—telephoning to say was everything all right?'

Embarrassed, Clare said she got this feeling, sometimes.

'What feeling?'

'Just this feeling that if I'm somewhere else the house can't be there any more.'

'I know,' said Maureen, surprisingly.

'Do you? You mean you've felt like that?'

'When I was a kid. Younger than you, mind, much. I ran all the way home from school, once, to see if my mum was still there. I got this idea all of a sudden she couldn't be, if I couldn't see her. Ever such a fuss there was—the teachers were in a proper state.'

'I thought it was just me,' said Clare.

'Nothing's ever just you. Take it from me. Nothing at all.'

The snow had been lying for days now, immobilised by frost. It was cleared from the roads and, here and there, from the pavements. Rigid grey heaps of it stood around at street corners and outside shops and front doors. Paths and uncleared pavements were furrowed with a thick, glassy skin: only where the city widened out into parks and playing-fields and gardens did it lie white and clean. At Norham Gardens the back garden was dark with birds, small, huddled shapes scavenging around the privet and among the clumps of dead stalks that pushed up from what had been flowerbeds. Clare threw bread out to them and stood at the open window, listening to the rush of their wings: the noise seemed unaccountably loud, like the calling of the rooks above the playing-fields. The city seemed to have contracted, to be cramped into a smaller space than usual. Purple clouds, heaped up around the horizon, were like distant mountains encircling it.

Maureen had a 'phone call from Weybridge, to say that her father was ill. She took a couple of days off and went home to see him.

Mrs Hedges caught 'flu from Linda. There was another telephone message to say she would not be in for a day or two. At school, Clare kept thinking of her. She rang the aunts to say she would go up to Headington on the bus, from school.

'That's a nice idea. You could take some flowers.'

'Yes . . .'

The flower shop in Summertown was showy with cinerarias, hyacinths, daffodils, chrysanthemums, all seasonally displaced and somehow inappropriate. Clare, staring at the banks of pots and trying to remember Mrs Hedges' favourite colour, and whether she preferred tulips or narcissi, felt as though someone had been interfering with the natural order of things, here, persuading plants that it was spring when it was not. It seemed profoundly unwise, to tamper with time itself. Reluctantly, she bought a pot of daffodils, green buds edged with yellow, and went out into the cold to wait at the bus stop, sheltering the flowers against her coat.

She got off the bus at the top of Headington Hill and walked through gathering darkness, down side-streets, to where Mrs Hedges lived. This was an estate of semi-detached houses with neat gardens and low, clipped hedges separating them from street and pavement. Norham Gardens was a grander, larger, more ornate ancestor to this kind of place. The houses blossomed in the twilight, their uncurtained windows orange and sometimes blue where television sets flickered in front rooms. They seemed, with the evening, to have taken on a magnetic quality—everywhere, people were homing on them: children scurrying in the shelter of walls and hedges, women pushing prams or carrying shopping bags, cars sweeping quietly round corners. Clare threaded her way through turnings to right and left, surprised by how easily she could find her way, in the dark, to a place she had only been to before by daylight.

Mrs Hedges came to the door in a dressing-gown, and at once began to scold.

'You shouldn't have come. All this way, and in filthy weather like this. And don't you get near me or you'll be having it next.'

Clare proffered the daffodils.

'Thanks. I love daffs. We'll put them in the warm and they'll be right out in a day or two. Nice to see them so early. Come on in and have some tea. It's Linda's half-day so she's home.'

Mrs Hedges was better, it seemed. She was watching television from the sofa. Linda made tea in the kitchen and shouted instructions at her mother through the hatch about keeping warm and not lifting a finger. Clare fed the goldfish and the bird and sat on a rug that Mrs Hedges had made last winter and felt—for the first time in many days—relaxed and comfortable. Linda came in with a tray of tea and scones she had just taken from the oven, and told Clare she had grown since the summer.

'I haven't, I'm sure, my clothes from last year still fit.'

'Then you've thinned out,' said Linda. 'That's it. Lost your puppy-fat. Growing up, isn't she, Mum?' They looked benevolently at Clare. 'Dad should be home.'

'Late shift,' said Mrs Hedges. 'The old ladies all right, are they? I don't like the thought of them on their own all day. Still, I'll be back, end of the week. Linda, bring the wedding dress down to show Clare.'

The dress, shrouded in tissue paper, was fetched and lay across the armchair like an object in a museum display. Dress, veil, shoes, sparkly arrangement for pinning veil to hair.

'What a commotion,' said Linda. 'All for one day. All that food and drink and a dress I won't ever wear again and I bet I'll be in such a state I'll never remember anything about it afterwards.'

''Course you will. It's something you look back on all your life. I remember every moment of mine.' Clare, following Mrs Hedges' glance, saw the framed photograph on the low table behind the sofa: Mr Hedges, young, in army uniform with three stripes on one sleeve and cap under the arm that was not threaded through that of the Linda/Mrs Hedges bride at his side, in a stiff square-shouldered jacket and skirt. No white tulle or sparkly head-dress.

'War-time,' said Mrs Hedges. 'Forty-eight hour leave, cider cup in the Village Hall, and a utility costume from the co-op that my mum gave me all her coupons for. And still I remember every minute.'

'You looked like Linda,' said Clare.

'Now then—who came first, may I ask? Linda looks like me, you mean.'

'Come off it,' said Linda. 'You're a stone heavier than I am.'

'That's middle age. Once upon a time I could have knocked spots off you, my girl. You ask your dad. Clare, if you don't eat that last scone no one else will.'

Linda drew the curtains. It was very warm, very companionable, with the smell of something meaty cooking in the kitchen and the budgerigar tapping at its reflection in a plastic mirror and Mrs Hedges talking on while she drank her tea. Clare sat listening and watching the ebb and flow of colours in the coke fire.

'... It seems a wretched time, when you think back, the war, and it was but we had our moments, all the same. Always waiting for something you seemed to be—weekend leaves, and letters, and a bit extra on the rations, or Christmas. And for when it would all be over, most of all. Always looking ahead, promising yourself things one day. They don't know they're born, nowadays, most of them. Shops crammed full of everything you could want, money to burn ...'

'I've been saving since I was seventeen,' said Linda indignantly.

'Oh, you're all right—you've been properly brought up, haven't you. And none of that winking at Clare—I can see you. All the same, there was something about things then that you don't get now—I couldn't put my finger on it, quite. Something about the way people would put themselves out for each other.'

'Spirit of the Blitz,' said Linda, yawning. 'I've seen old war films, too.'

Mrs Hedges told Linda off for being cheeky about things she didn't understand and Linda teased her mother for being nostalgic and the budgerigar clicked and tapped and sprayed bird-seed on to the carpet. Mrs Hedges put her feet up on the sofa and talked about Saturday night dances at the Naafi and working in a munitions factory and being a landgirl and about D-day and VE night, and Clare listened and dozed and sat up with a start when the clock on the mantelpiece struck seven.

'Is it really as late as that? I've been gone hours—I should go back.'

'That was Mrs Enid Hedges' short course in Twentieth Century History,' said Linda. 'Six easy lessons.'

'Take no notice,' said Mrs Hedges. 'It's gone to her head, all this getting married. Thank you for coming over, dear—it's cheered me up. Tell the old ladies I'll see them Friday, probably.'

'Yes. Thanks for the scones. Goodnight.'

'Goodnight. Take care how you go. Get the bus at the traffic lights.'

It was freezing hard. Clare, turning the corner into the main road, slipped on the icy pavement and nearly fell. The black roads glinted where car headlights raked down them. Riding through the city on the bus was like being carried in a warm, steamy tank. You rubbed the window and the grey mist turned to water, running down the glass, and beyond were shops and people and lights, all slightly elongated, blurring into each other like images in trick mirrors at a fairground. It made you want to travel along like this for ever, passive, not bothering about anything, making no decisions. Clare sat, lethargic, thinking of nothing, and went past her stop. She had to walk back, down Banbury Road, getting cold again.

She opened the front door into darkness. So unexpected was this that she jumped as though the black hall were something solid, a wall that you could knock yourself out against. Her first, confused thought, then, was that there was an electricity cut. She shouted, and no one answered. The house, now that she had shut the door, swallowed her, empty, apparently, and pitch dark. She felt, for an instant, quite panic-stricken, and then groped for the light switches, and the hall light came on, and the one on the landing above. She called again, 'Aunt Susan! Here I am—I'm back!' and threw the library door open, and it was dark in there, now, with the curtains not drawn and the fire not lit, never having been lit, the ashes quite cold. She stood there for a moment, and the most awful feeling came in her stomach, and her heart began to thump, and she went out again and ran past the hall table, knocking some letters off it and a sheet of white paper that fluttered to the floor and got under her foot and made her skid as she rushed up the stairs, calling. John's room was empty—it would be, of course, he was going to a late class, she remembered now—and Maureen was still away. And there was no one anywhere. Every room was empty. The bedrooms, the drawing-room, the dining-room, the study. Empty, quite empty. No one there at all.

She came down the stairs again talking in her head, or, quite possibly, out loud. 'They never go out. They haven't been out for weeks. They wouldn't go out when it's snowy like this.' She went into the kitchen and everything was tidy and put away—no cups or plates on the table or anything left about. The tap dripping. The clock ticking too loud.

'Aunt Susan! Aunt Anne!' Back into the hall. Standing there, crying, almost. Something's happened. There's been an accident. Things were unreeling in her mind—pictures, not words, flashed images that she didn't want to see. The aunts hurt, ill ... She went back into the kitchen, to shut the pictures out, and then into the library, and back into the hall again. She picked the telephone up, held it for a moment, put it down again. Stood for a moment, again, with a cold, drained feeling going all through her and then ran out of the house, leaving the front door open, and down the steps and out of the drive and up the steps of Mrs Rider's house. The door was open and she went straight in—into the hall that was a twin to her own but entirely different, with plastic-tiled floor and racks of pigeon-holes for letters and a green baize notice-board. A girl student came out of one of the rooms and Clare said, 'Please—is Mrs Rider here?' and the girl went through to the kitchen and then came back and said, 'No, sorry,' and went upstairs.

Clare went back to the house. She ran up the steps and through the open door and up the stairs and into each room, again, praying in her head to open a door and find them sitting there and everything all right, a mistake, a bad dream ... But the house was empty; still. They weren't there, and this was happening, it was perfectly real.

She couldn't, she knew, be by herself like this any more. She had to find someone to help. Mrs Hedges. I need Mrs Hedges. But she hasn't got a telephone—I'll have to go up there. The bus takes too long. Bike. I'll go by bike. Mrs Hedges and Linda will help. They'll know what to do.

She rode too fast, standing up on the pedals, and the wheels kept swerving about in a funny way as though perhaps there was something wrong with the tyres and going round into Banbury Road she slid into the pavement and saved herself from falling with one foot. She went straight down Banbury Road and then when she got to the corner of Keble Road she remembered that it would be much quicker not to go through the town, but round by South Parks Road, that way, to Longwall, so she swerved quickly to get round the corner.

And the bike floated away, somehow, sideways, and she went with it, not able to stop it, and there was an awful noise just behind, a car's brakes squealing, and she was lying on her back on the road, and the bike or something was on top of her. Everything was quite clear now, and calm, not all anxious and spinning like a few minutes ago. She was lying on her back on the road, and a man was getting out of a car and there were some people running towards her and for some reason she just went on lying there. And another part of her seemed to be watching, as though this had happened to someone else, not her.

The people were looking down at her now and someone said, 'It's all right—don't move,' and a man put a coat over her and she thought she should say thank you but for some odd reason she wasn't able to. And she ought to get up, not just lie there on the road, but she couldn't do that either, because the part of her that was outside, watching, was the only part that could decide things. The person lying on the road could only hear cars going past and people's voices, and the sound their feet made moving around her on the road. A man said, 'The ambulance should be here in a moment,' and a woman's voice, very close, right over her said, 'I wonder who she is.'

The other Clare, the watcher, wanted to tell them, but somehow she was going further and further away now, up and up, above the road and the trees, and after a while she wasn't in the same place at all. She was in some kind of space-ship, a bubble of plastic which turned over and over, floating aimlessly in a sky without a horizon. The bubble had no up and no down, no top and no bottom: it revolved aimlessly and sickeningly, tumbling in space, and she, the person inside it, scrabbled at the transparent walls and tumbled with it, now on her stomach, now on her back, sliding over the smooth surface that offered no hold of any kind, no handle or ledge or rope. She spun, and the bubble spun and the featureless sky spun around it, and she could not get out, and it would not stop.

CHAPTER 11 _____

*One day, visitors come again to the tribe. This time,
they weigh them, and measure their height, and count
their teeth, and peer into their eyes. They are asked
their age (which they do not know) and their names,
and the names of their husband and their wife and
their father and mother. Their throats are examined,
and their finger-nails, and the soles of their feet. They
are injected and vaccinated and dosed with medicines.
The tribe have arrived in the twentieth century. They
have no ritual for the celebration of such an event, because it has never happened before, so they remain
silent.*

Clare was lying on her back on a bed that someone was wheeling
along. Her head hurt. She hurt all over. The bed stopped moving
and a man was looking down at her. He smiled. 'Don't worry,' he
said, 'soon have you all fixed up. You're just going off to sleep for
a bit now.'

She did not feel sleepy, and was about to tell him so, and then,
strangely, a kind of blackness began to come up from behind her
eyes, and she fought against it, but it was huge, swallowing her,
taking her away, and there was nothing she could do. She gave in,
and went with it, into darkness.

She was in Burford church, walking among those high, light cliffs
of stone. The names were scored deeply into the stone: In Memory
of ..., In Fond Remembrance ..., Pray for the Soul of ... She

walked slowly, reading, because you must not leave this place until you have done so, though there was, she knew, something else, perhaps more important, that she had to do. The tamburan was under her arm, wrapped in an old tweed jacket that came also from the attic. It had been great-grandfather's and smelled comfortingly of tobacco, though there were moth-holes in it and the lining was almost in shreds. It was not an ideal covering as the arms kept unwrapping and she would have to stop to re-arrange it around the tamburan. It was remarkable how the colours had come up lately: it was quite brilliant now, dazzling, almost, as though it had been made yesterday. It reminded her of the paintings in a medieval church she had once seen restored to their original brilliance—blazing and, in some obscure way, quite inappropriate as though to do such a thing were to tamper not with the painting but with time itself. The tamburan was rather like that now: its brightness was quite disturbing which was one reason why she had to wrap it in the old jacket.

The church door was open and outside, as she had known, lay dense green jungle and, quite close, the abrupt slope of the mountain side, reaching up, blue and billowing with tree-tops, to a sky packed with white cloud. She was going to have to climb, this time, before she could reach the people, and it looked as though it would take some time, and probably be hard work. She hitched the tamburan up under her arm and looked for a way through the trees that began where the bamboo ended, small, scrubby trees first but becoming higher and taller and denser, she could see, further up the mountain.

There was a track, quite well worn, as though others had been this way, and she started up it, following its twists and curves as it avoided fallen trees, wet places, and the steepest gradients of the mountainside. Ahead of her, and invisible, there were sudden manic bird-noises, shrieks and screams: sound would explode far away up in the tree-tops, the flap of wings, leaves and branches moving. The path was quite wide and definite, and not yet very steep, and she fancied that she could see the prints of other feet in the dirt and leaf-mould. There was no one about, though, and neither did she expect there to be: this, she had always known, was a journey to be taken alone. There were flowers in the shadowy places at the edge of the path—the kind of greenish and whitish flowers that grow in places without much light, larger and more emphatic versions of the spurges and anemones of English woods. Once or twice she stopped to look at them, and saw butterflies, too, like dappled, moving shadows. So far, the climb was not unpleasant.

But it was beginning to get steeper. Steeper and darker and wetter. There was a faint, clammy mist so that in places where the trunks of the trees thinned out and she could see a few yards into the forest the light was dim and blue. And the tree trunks themselves were furred over with green moss, so that they soared up on all sides of her as great emerald columns, reaching up and up to a vaulting of leaves from which moisture pattered down on to her head and on to the path. It was like walking, climbing, through some huge damp cathedral.

The path had got narrower, and seemed to have been less frequented here: several times she had to stop to push aside hanging curtains of a parasitic plant that slung itself round the trunks and branches of the trees, or to climb over a huge, decaying log that lay right across the path. There were no butterflies now: the insect life upon the path or on the branches level with her head was all of the creeping, crawling or writhing variety so that she preferred not to look too closely, and kept her arms pinned close to her sides and her head down. The flowers, where they occurred, were orchids. Greenhouse orchids in pale, luminous colours, hanging from branches and boles like serpents, waxen and gently swaying. She thought them unattractive and wondered why people went to such pains to grow them, in botanical gardens and hothouses.

There were no birds now. Nothing lived here, it seemed, except creeping things. Once, looking down, she saw something black and slug-like sticking to her leg, and brushed it away with the back of her hand, shuddering uncontrollably. The leeches of which great-grandfather had spoken ... She tried to hurry, still shuddering, but the path was very steep now, rising almost sheer through the squelching leaf-mould, and she was out of breath, her heart racing and ears pounding. She kept slipping, too, on the wet track, coming down on to her knees and scrambling up again in a panic, with a horrid fear of what might rise up from the path with her. Leeches, nastiness ... There was so much water coming down from the trees now that it could more fairly be called rain than mist, and the air itself was so dense with moisture that she could hardly see two yards ahead of her. It was as though she climbed up the very course of a waterfall.

And it got colder and colder. She unwrapped the tamburan from great-grandfather's coat and put the coat on—it did not seem any longer important to suppress the brilliance of the colours and she had no fear that the water would spoil the wood. The coat, of course, was too big for her: the sleeves flapped to her finger-tips and the hem of it reached to her thighs, but it felt reassuring and she was able to get along faster for a while, though the going seemed to become harder and harder. And there was no way of telling how near or how far she might be from the summit. That was the worst of it. On an ordinary, unclothed mountain that at least would be clear, but in this twilit forest she might be nowhere near the top, or a few yards away, and be none the wiser. There was nothing for it but to struggle on.

On and up. She must have climbed very high now, she thought. Thousands of feet? Maybe the pounding in her ears had something to do with that, as well as the physical effort of the climb. Maybe she was so high above sea level that the oxygen was thin. With this thought came a little rush of panic—a feeling that she would never make it, might as well give up ... Several times she hesitated and half turned back, but each time something drove her on. You've got so far, she told herself, you've put up with leeches and got wet through and out of breath, you can't give up now. And they're waiting ... And then, quite suddenly, the blue curtain of mist ahead of her became opaque, with something lying beyond that was not trees nor mountainside but something altogether light and bright and different. Sunshine. There was a rainbow of colour all around her, and the incessant patter of the drops from the trees had stopped, and in a moment the trees themselves, and the ground, no longer went upwards in front of her but had levelled off and fell away steeply down.

Down into the valley. She was on a ridge, with the trees behind and in front the wide and placid valley, neatly chequered with their fields and dotted with the little squat thatched buttons of their huts, clustered about thin blue whiskers of smoke from their cooking-fires. The valley was a great green bowl, floored with the delicate patchwork patterning of their fields, safely cradled between the blue swell of the mountains all around—the mountains up which she had struggled for what, now, seemed hours. Up here, they were no longer so daunting: the mist had gone and there were only harmless puffs of white cloud lying along the skyline, and a clear turquoise sky. She began to go down into the valley, noticing as she did so that there was some curious brown scarring among the fields of the valley that she could not for the moment identify. Thick brown lines that, here and there, cut a swathe right through the patchwork of the fields.

The descent did not take long, through light scrub and, lower down, springy turf dotted about with big grey boulders. There were butterflies again, and birds singing, and the distant noise of dogs barking and once or twice men shouting. There was another noise, too, as she got lower and into the valley itself—a rhythmic throbbing that seemed somehow to have no place here. She tightened her grip on the tamburan and hurried. She was still wearing the coat and though it was warm down here—hot, even—she thought that it would be better to keep it on.

Down in the valley, she was soon in among bamboo and pandanus, head-high, hurrying along the kind of twisting, much used path that now seemed familiar. She could still hear that throbbing noise, somewhere quite near now, and thought, disbelievingly, that it sounded like an engine of some kind. Leaving the bamboo and coming to a more open stretch, with fields and gardens, she found herself right on top of the brown scarring she had seen from above. It was as though a giant claw had reached down into the valley and scraped a wide track right across it. It was, she recognised with amazement, the basic construction of a road.

She crossed the dry, rutted channel—it had the broad herring-boning of tyre-marks on it, she now saw—and went into another bamboo plantation. She thought she must be very near the village now and began to run. She felt certain also that she had been far too long in coming. Far, far too long.

She came out of the bamboo and into the clearing where the village had been. But the huts had gone. In their place were neat ranks of small concrete bungalows, facing each other across a dusty road. One of them was a shop, with tattered advertisements for Coca Cola and washing powder and various brands of cigarettes plastered across its verandah, and another sprouted an arrangement of wires and poles that must have to do with radio transmission. There was a battered and dusty lorry standing at the far end of the bungalow, and a couple of bicycles leaning against the wall of the shop.

They were there, squatted down in the wedges of shadow at the foot of the bungalow walls, or leaning on window sills, or walking down the road. The men wore shirts and khaki shorts, and most of them had cigarette stubs in the corners of their mouths, or tucked behind an ear. The women had cotton dresses on. Only one or two of the very small children went naked. Nobody took any notice at all of Clare. She could walk up to them and their eyes would rove across her, and the jacket, and the tamburan, and rove away again, impassive. They all seemed apathetic, and as though they either had nothing to do or no inclination to do what should be done. In front of the shop a group of the men were clustered around something, huddled over it in silence. Going up to them, and leaning over them, she saw that it was a transistor radio. They stared intently at it and one of them fiddled with the knobs. It howled and whistled and then an English voice came out, with an accent she could not place, reading a news bulletin.

It was moments before she could attract their attention, force them to look up from the radio which seemed to mesmerise them, as though if they did not look at it they would not be able to hear it. 'Look,' she kept saying, 'please look,' and she held the tamburan out, face towards them, with all its colours bright and sharp, and still they would not look, hunched there over the radio.

But in the end they did, turning towards her and looking first at her, without interest and then, at last, at the tamburan. One of them reached out an arm in a tattered cotton sleeve and held it and stared at it and then he shook his head, to and fro, blankly, and handed it back to her. 'The time is six p.m. Western Australia time,' said the voice on the radio. 'Time for Music Roundup,' and music crackled out into the sunshine and the valley and the high clear sky and the men turned away from her and crouched down over the radio again and left her standing there, holding out the tamburan, not knowing what she should do next.

She came up through a great many layers of white fog saying, 'They don't want it any more.'

She was in bed. There were screens around the bed and some-one's arm, all wrapped up in white but with bare fingers most oddly protruding at the end, was lying in front of her face, and a woman in a white cap was standing beside the bed. The woman smiled and said, 'There you are, then. Back with us again. How do you feel now, dear?'

A nurse. This is a hospital. That's my arm.

'What's happened to my arm?' said Clare.

'You had a nasty fall off your bike, dear. One broken arm and some bruises and a bang on the head.'

'Am I going to stay here long?'

'Just till we're sure your head's all right.'

'I feel sick.'

Hours later, she woke from another, different, sleep, and things began to fall into place. It was the next day. The aunts would be coming along to see her soon. No, there was nothing at all the matter with them: what had made her think there might be? Her arm would be in plaster for some time. She could go home in a day or two, when the doctor had seen her again. There would be fish for lunch. The weather had improved.

People in hospitals are like refugees. Detached from their own lives, they establish new relationships, create a new world for themselves, fence themselves in with new concerns. By the after-noon Clare's closest friend was the lady in the next bed who had fallen off the step-ladder in the kitchen and damaged herself in various ways. She had four grandchildren and before the lunch came round on clanking trolleys Clare knew a great deal about them all, and a great many other things besides. Her view of the outside world was limited to six squares of sky let into the opposite wall of the ward, and the most immediate and interesting thing was the glass door at the end through which came and went everything that was worth watching. It was something of a shock when, eventually, it opened to admit the aunts, looking bewildered and concerned.

Explanations. A note. On the hall table. Old friend, who had called, with car, and insisted on taking aunts out to expensive dinner. 'Against our better judgement,' said Aunt Susan. 'I am so sorry ...'

A piece of white paper, getting under the feet, while one was dashing around, not being sensible ...

'No,' said Clare. 'I was stupid. Absolutely daft. Mad.'

'We didn't even enjoy the dinner particularly,' said Aunt Anne. 'Much too rich. My poor girl ... How are you?'

'It's a funny thing, but in fact I feel better than I have for ages. Kind of clear in the head. Has it stopped snowing?'

'Yes. Indeed, there seems to be a thaw on the way. But had you been unclear? You should have told us.'

'It wasn't anything you could explain to anyone, really. Just a feeling. When am I coming home?'

'Soon. They want to observe you for a day or two.'

More visitors came. Mrs Cramp. Liz. Mrs Hedges. Maureen and John, together, John's face staring gravely over the top of pink chrysanthemums that bulged like icecream from a cone of white paper. They sat on either side of the bed and contemplated her. Clare felt priest-like, as though she had only to reach out and take them both by the hand, to unite them for ever. 'Wilt thou take this woman ...' A weak giggle escaped her and Maureen said sternly, 'You shouldn't get yourself excited. Rest, you need.' In a lower voice, but not low enough, as though accidents impaired people's hearing, she said to John, 'We shouldn't stay too long. Better be off in a minute.' John nodded.

She went home, sitting up in an ambulance like a little bus, her plastered arm in a sling. Something had happened to the outside world while she had been away. It had turned green and brown. The snow had all gone, except for islands of white that lingered here and there on lawns or paths, and grey humps in gutters or beside lamp-posts. The roads were wet and black, the trees dripping, the sky pale blue, arching high and wide above the city. Everything seemed brightly coloured—the red brick houses, green grass, the shiny brown buds tipping the chestnut branches that overhung a wall. Going up the steps at Norham Gardens, she noticed the blunt tips of crocuses poking up through the grass at the side of the house, purple and yellow. They must have been there all the time, underneath the snow, and one hadn't known about them. Forgotten they were there.

Home, she toured the house, as though she had been away for a long time and needed to make sure that everything was all right and in its proper place. Drawing-room, library, study, dining-room, spare rooms. She tidied her own room, excavating drawers and cupboards, filling cardboard boxes with rubbish, laboriously, with one hand, arranging books according to subject and author. She threw out the chair she had always used at her desk and asked John to help her bring up the one from the study, a heavy, dark brown thing with a leather seat, that swivelled on its base. Great-grandfather had used it.

'Why all these changes, suddenly?'

'I'm spring-cleaning,' said Clare.

Mrs Hedges, emptying the cardboard boxes into the dustbin, said, 'Trust you to wait till you've got a broken arm, and then decide to turn the place upside down.'

Liz came round after school, and was swept up to the attic, to help with a clearing-out process. Clare had emptied all the things out of the trunks on to the floor, and was sorting them out, folding them, and wrapping the more elaborate dresses in paper, putting them carefully away again. Liz trundled to and fro obediently.

'Those can be thrown away,' said Clare. 'Those old shoes. I'm only keeping the most important things.'

'What about this? Kind of hairy jacket thing? For a man.'

'No. That's to be kept.'

'You couldn't possibly want it for anything.'

'It was useful once,' said Clare briskly. 'Put it in there, with the dresses. There, that's much better.' She looked round the room with satisfaction. 'Now you know where everything is.'

'What about that nasty shield thing?'

'It isn't nasty, it's very interesting. I'll be seeing about that in a day or two. Let's go down and have tea.'

'Does your arm hurt?'

'Not now. It tickles inside the plaster, though. I hope I can have it off before the holidays, if we're going on this cycling trip.'

'I thought you weren't interested.'

'I am now,' said Clare.

There was something else to be done, also. On Saturday it would be Aunt Susan's birthday. I am going, Clare thought, to buy her a very special present. Not anything she needs, but something she didn't at all know that she wanted. But something that, as soon as she sees it, she will know she couldn't possibly do without. It was a large ambition: going out of the front door, she had no idea how she would set about fulfilling it.

First, though, she had to see the doctor. The hospital had said that she must, and Mrs Hedges had rung the surgery.

Clare walked up Banbury Road with her coat hugged round her, one arm flapping loose. In the surgery, she attracted sympathetic glances. A woman chivvied her small boy off his seat to give her somewhere to sit down. The receptionist had a cold: her nose was fringed with pink and her voice, snapping orders at the patients, was thick and resentful. Clare smiled cosily at her and she looked away, uncomfortable.

The doctor was reading a letter from the hospital.

'Well, now,' he said, 'skidded on the ice, I hear.'

'Yes.'

'Not too much damage, though. Arm going on all right?'

'Yes, thank you.'

'Head not aching at all? No sickness?'

'No. I'm feeling very well.'

'Bruises?'

'They're going.'

'Splendid.' The doctor looked down at the paper in front of him. 'How's this sleeping business? Any better?'

'Much better.'

'That's the idea,' said the doctor. 'Jolly good. Well, come along and see me in a week or two, then '

'Yes,' said Clare. 'Thank you. Goodbye.'

Outside again, she hesitated. A bus, headed for the town, was just drawing up at the stop and for a moment she thought of taking it, and then changed her mind. One thing was certain, and that was that an appropriate present for Aunt Susan would not be found in the bright and all-providing shops of the town. She wandered along the pavement uncertainly for a while, and then remembered the cluster of antique and junk shops in the back streets beyond the hospital. Maybe she could look around there and find something.

There were several shops, all identically murky as though someone felt a deliberate gloom appropriate to the display of old or beautiful objects. The first one only had furniture in it, and in the second the vases and pieces of silver on show were arranged with a care that made them likely to be much too expensive. The third, in which things were stacked, rather than arranged, was more promising.

She went in. The shop was full of tables, each one covered with objects. More objects filled bookcases and shelves: pictures and mirrors covered the walls. She had been standing there for several minutes, looking around, when a movement at the back of the shop became a woman, who must have been there all the time, like some creature with protective colouring, inert among the shadows. 'Is there anything you're interested in, particularly?'

Clare had opened a leather-covered box. There were initials on the lid, engraved in silver: V. M. B. Inside, a silver toilet set. It was worn. Someone had used this, once, day after day.

'Fifty pounds,' said the woman.

'Yes.' Clare shut the box.

'Were you looking for anything in particular?'

'A present ...'

There were old flat-irons, polished up, with white price tickets on the handles. At Norham Gardens, on the larder shelf, there was one like that, without a price ticket. The price tickets said one pound fifty pence. For one pound fifty you can remember what it was like before people had electric irons. Beyond the irons, miscellaneous objects filled a dark corner. A sewing-machine for six pounds. A gramophone for eight. Knife boxes, stone crocks, boxes of faded postcards, one of those white hats for tropical wear, the lining stained with sweat.

The woman said, 'That's not antiques there, of course. Just old things. There's a big demand for that kind of thing, now.'

'Oh,' said Clare. She picked up a beaded purse, and put it down again. Seventy pence.

'Have a look round.'

Oil lamps. For three pounds fifty pence you could dispense with electric light. For two seventy-five you could remember the war with a gas mask. Neat round labels priced each object of survival: the older they were, the more expensive. Candlesticks, pieces of embroidery, pictures. A dark landscape was labelled 'Nineteenth century. £45.' For forty-five pounds you could buy your own two square feet of the nineteenth century. Clare began to move towards the door. 'There's some cheaper things in the other room. Quite nice for presents.'

'Thank you. Actually—well, I'm not sure this person really needs anything like that.'

'Most people like something old, these days. It's fashionable, having old things.'

'Thank you for letting me look,' said Clare. She edged out of the door.

'You're welcome.'

Clare closed the door behind her and walked away. Crossing the road, she saw someone else go into the shop. Perhaps the woman would be able to sell him something old, for ninety pence, or three pounds fifty, or forty-five pounds. Old things were fashionable.

All of a sudden she knew what Aunt Susan wanted for her birthday.

CHAPTER 12

Houses are built for the tribe, and roads. They learn how to drive cars, use telephones, tin-openers, matches and screwdrivers. They are given laws which they must obey: they are not to kill one another and they must pay their taxes. They listen to the radio and they make no more tamburans, but their nights are rich with dreams. The children of the tribe learn how to read and write: they sit at wooden desks with their heads bent low over sheets of paper, and make marks on the paper. One day, they will discover again the need for tamburans, and they will make a new kind of tamburan for themselves, and for their children, and their children's children.

She carried it back sloped over her shoulder, the roots tidily shrouded in black plastic. It seemed dry and lifeless but there were, she could see, very small dark swellings at the end of its thin branches. Maureen, coming downstairs on her way out, was amazed.

'But that's going to take years to grow. Years and years.'

'I know. About fifty, the man in the shop said. And then it'll last another two or three hundred, if people don't interfere with it.'

'A rose bush she'd get more out of,' said Maureen doubtfully. 'A nice standard rose.'

Clare said, 'No. A tree is what she'd like. A copper beech, this is. In summer it has those dark red leaves and you can lie underneath and look up through them and it's as though the sky was on fire.'

'Well,' said Maureen, 'it's an original present—I'll say that.'

They planted the tree on Aunt Susan's birthday, ceremoniously, at the end of a bright and sunny afternoon that had brought the crocuses out. They were still glowing now, though the sun had gone down and twilight seemed to seep up, somehow, from the ground itself, like the mists that sometimes crept off the river and up the streets. John dug a hole, at the far end of the garden, and Aunt Susan lowered the clutch of roots into it. She had been delighted with her present. It reminded her, apparently, of a tree she had liked long ago, in the garden of some house in Somerset where the aunts had stayed. The aunts argued, amiably, about the name of the people who had owned the house, and the year in which they had visited them.

'Never mind,' said Aunt Susan, 'it's the tree I remember best, anyway. How nice that I am giving birth to one like it, as it were.'

'Excuse me,' said John, staring down at the tree, 'it does not look to me very well.'

'Why?' Clare and the aunts looked at him, and back at the tree.

'It is like a stick. No leaves.'

They laughed. Clare explained about English trees losing their leaves in winter which African ones, it seemed, did not. John, impressed, examined the leaf-buds, and seemed to find the whole process remarkable.

'Whatever had you thought?' said Aunt Anne. 'You must have imagined the whole landscape dying around you.'

'I am a most unobservant person,' said John. 'I hadn't even thought about it.'

Mrs Hedges had made a birthday cake. It had a single candle in the middle. 'Is this tact?' said Aunt Susan. 'Or an insufficiency of candles? What a very kind thought, though.'

'People are kind,' said Clare. 'The people I know, anyway. Mrs Hedges, and Maureen, and John, and Mrs Cramp at school. Cousin Margaret, even.'

'What a benevolent girl you are. Do be careful—stoking the fire with one arm like that.'

'I am being. It's funny what a lot of things you don't need two arms for. Why am I benevolent?'

'Finding people kind.'

'Aren't they?'

'Individually, yes,' said Aunt Susan. 'Collectively, seldom. Have a slice of my cake.'

They ate cake in front of the fire, and the fire wheezed and shifted and sighed and outside the wall at the end of the garden turned black and the sky a hard midnight blue.

'Draw the curtains,' said Aunt Anne, 'there's a dear. Or does that need two arms?'

'No. One does fine.' Clare stood at the window for a moment and looked down the long tunnel of the garden. She could just see the tree, looking young and forlorn with the earth roughed up round its feet, and beyond it the bed where the Christmas roses grew. Not long ago she had picked them and stood looking back at the house and everything had seemed unreal. There had been people where now there were only the dark stiff branches of the chestnut in Mrs Rider's garden, and voices where now the black strands of the telephone wires swooped across the wall. And in dreams she'd walked straight through that wall and into another country. The dreams, though, had been interesting. She couldn't really remember them, except that the same people had kept coming into them, and they had seemed in some curious way to be telling a story. And the story seemed to be finished now. She came and sat down by the fire again.

'Any more cake?'

Cousin Margaret wrote to say what frightfully bad luck about the arm and she hoped Aunt Anne's cold was better. Sal, she said, was not going to the family in France any more because actually she and Edwin thought perhaps she needed to stand on her own feet a bit so she was going to do a secretarial course in Ipswich instead. Bumpy had lost more teeth. They were looking forward to seeing Clare in August.

The sun shone. A sun with more brilliance than warmth but that nevertheless disposed of the last snow patches and the grey clumps of ice on street corners, and opened out the crocuses and brought the daffodils up in the school flowerbeds. It was nearly March, Clare was surprised to find, looking at the calendar over the kitchen sink.

'Spring,' said Maureen, staring out of the window. 'I never know about spring, whether I like it or not.'

'I do. It's the beginning of something. Anything might happen.'

'Mmn. When you've seen a few of them, though, it never seems long since the last one. And nothing much ever has happened.' She tightened the belt of her dressing-gown and went away upstairs. The dressing-gown came downstairs again now, regardless of John, and she had stopped bothering to put lipstick on at breakfast. She talked to John in an ordinary voice, too. Clare remembered her thoughts when Maureen and John had visited her in hospital, and told him about them.

'When I was in hospital I imagined you and Maureen getting married.'

'Do you think that would be a good idea?' said John politely.

'Not really, I suppose.'

'No,' said John. 'Anyway I don't think she would want to marry me. Though she is a very nice person,' he added.

Clare, feeling that she had brought order into the house, at least in so far as this was possible, turned her attention from her bedroom and the attic to the garden. She found a rusting trowel and fork in the shed and went out. Everything was very wet and she felt there was a great deal that ought to be done, without exactly knowing what. She cut some dead wood out of a climbing rose, and pulled up some obvious weeds, leaving other, more doubtful things that she did not feel competent to classify. Gardening with one arm was not easy: it required a certain inventiveness. There were noises from the other side of the wall and Mrs Rider's head appeared.

'Hello, there. I didn't know you were keen on gardening.'

'I'm not,' said Clare, 'I just felt it seemed to need arranging. How do you tell which are weeds and which are plants?'

'If it's strong-growing and looks at home,' said Mrs Rider, 'you can be sure it's a weed. As often as not.' She peered over the wall.

'That's a michaelmas daisy, by your foot. You want to leave that. How's the old ladies?'

'Very well thank you. Aunt Anne's cold is much better.'

'That's good,' said Mrs Rider. 'Inconvenient for them, though, that big house. All the stairs.'

'Not really. They like it. They've lived there a long time.'

'That's a point,' said Mrs Rider vaguely. She gave Clare a sharp look and said, 'You're looking better yourself, I'd say. Very peaky I thought you were last time I saw you. Been overdoing it at school, I daresay.'

'Yes. I expect that's what it was '

The garden, after an hour or so, did look neater. She gave some water to the tree, which seemed to be settling down, and went inside, feeling pleased with herself. There was something else to be done that she had been saving up for the right moment, when she felt like doing it, and now all of a sudden the right moment seemed to have come. She put on a coat, changed her shoes, which had got muddy in the garden, and went up to the attic. She came downstairs with the tamburan tucked under her arm.

She met John at the front door, coming in.

'Hello. Where are you taking your shield?'

'I'm going to give it to the museum.'

'Ah. Won't you miss it, though? You were so interested in it.'

'I think I've finished with it,' said Clare. 'Or it's finished with me. It would be safer in a museum, if it's very special.'

'You are probably right.'

'If it can't be where it belongs, then a museum is the best place.'

John went upstairs, and Clare walked down Norham Gardens and past the Parks. Everything shone. The grass was brightly green and the earth a sticky brown and the melting snow had left a wet sheen over everything. The road was black and gleaming and the parked cars glittered in the sun. Clare carried the tamburan face outwards under her arm but nobody looked at it, and this gave her an elusive feeling of the same thing having happened once before, somewhere else. Passing the two or three Victorian houses that survived among the new buildings beside the Parks she had another, equally evasive, memory of having seen them, also, under other circumstances. Both impressions occupied her mind until she reached the entrance to the museum, and then she forgot all about them.

To walk into a museum carrying under your arm an object which clearly belongs there is a disconcerting experience. Like, Clare thought, shoplifting in reverse. She walked by the various people in the Natural History Museum feeling acutely uncomfortable: the student on a camp stool, drawing the blue whale's skeleton, and the clutch of small boys staring at pickled jellyfish, seemed to follow her with their eyes as she hurried past. As for Prince Albert, Darwin and the rest, on their marble plinths . . .

Once inside the Pitt Rivers, she anticipated any attack that might come by marching straight up to the attendant. She had not rehearsed what she would say and heard herself being embarrassingly incoherent. The attendant looked sideways at the tamburan, with surprise, and then at her, with doubt.

'You want to see someone about giving something to the museum?'

Clare nodded. The attendant disappeared for a moment through a door into some private, inner world of the museum and came back with another man.

He examined the tamburan. 'Very nice. Lovely. But where on earth did you get it?'

Clare explained.

'How extraordinary,' said the man. 'Of course we'd like it, though. It can go with the rest of the Mayfield Collection.' He ran his hand over the surface of the tamburan. 'How very bright it is. In better condition than our own, really. It could have been made yesterday. Has it been stored with special care?'

'No. Just in a trunk in the attic.'

'Really? Well—many thanks. Would you like to wait while I write out a receipt. What did you say your name was?'

'Clare Mayfield.'

'We could label it "Donated by Miss Clare Mayfield".'

Clare, going hot and red about the face, said, 'Thank you very much.' The man was looking at the tamburan again. He held it in front of him, with both hands, and looked at it with detachment, like a scientist observing remote forms of life under a microscope. 'Extraordinarily powerful images, these things,' he said. 'New Guinea's not really my field, but one can't help being fascinated by them. Your great-grandfather acquired it himself, you say?'

'Yes.'

'Interesting. The tribes were usually very reluctant to part with them. They had a deep magical significance, you see.'

'I know,' said Clare. 'They wanted it back for a long time and then things happened to them and they didn't any more. They forgot why they'd needed them.'

The man stared at her, perplexed. 'What?'

Clare went red again. 'Nothing. Sorry. I think I'd better go home now.'

'Well,' said the man, 'many thanks.' They smiled at each other, awkwardly, and the man went away into his private part of the museum again, taking the tamburan with him. Clare watched it go without emotion. She thought that she might come to visit it when it had been arranged somewhere, in a glass case, or on the stairs with the others, and then again she might not. There would be no particular need to, because she was never likely to forget it, though it had lost the urgency it once had for her. It would be rather fun, though, to see her name on a label, if that man had meant what he said.

Leaving the museum, she remembered that the last time she had gone home from there she had taken John with her. He had met Aunt Susan, and eaten digestive biscuits in front of the fire. It had been snowing and he had been a stranger. Now, the sun was out and John was someone she seemed to have known for a very long time. People you like seem always to have been there: you forget about the time when they were not. She walked back along Parks Road under a blue sky that was both above and below her at the same time—overhead, fringed with trees and houses, and underneath, plunging below the road, the same landscape in reverse shining up from the puddles. Safely tethered to the road, she walked in the middle of this circular world, looking down into the water and enjoying the oddness of her own reflection, foreshortened, feet first, upside-down in a floating mirror. It reminded her, for some reason, of the chameleon in the zoo, but its bifocal view of the world had seemed, at the time, unbearably disconcerting. Now, from a firm standpoint in the centre of things, it was not. She stamped in a puddle, childishly, for the fun of shattering sky, trees and houses and watching them re-assemble.

In the evening she sat in the library with the aunts, at the heart of the silent house. John and Maureen had both gone out. Sitting by the fire, Clare thought of the rooms of the houses, stacked around her, empty and yet full. Maureen's room, and John's, would be full of their possessions, for as long as they lived here, and, thus, of them. Photographs, clothes, books. When, in time, they went away, would anything remain of them here, as so much remained of great-grandfather and great-grandmother and the whole long lives of the aunts? Not really, Clare thought, except for me, because I knew them. Where they will be, in a peculiar way, is inside my head, but I'm the only person who'll know about that. All the same, that's important—going on inside someone else's head.

'Lost in thought,' said Aunt Susan, 'as usual. How is the arm?'

'Tickling.'

There was a flurry of newspaper as Aunt Anne tried to arrange the page she wanted in a satisfactory reading position. Aunt Susan sighed. 'The only thing,' she said, 'well, one of the only things—I have always held against Anne is her daily massacre of newspapers. In all my life, I have hardly ever picked up a clean, uncrumpled newspaper.'

'It's a small martyrdom,' said Aunt Anne, 'compared to most.' They grinned at each other over Clare's head.

'And you?' said Aunt Susan. 'Child—Clare—What are your private grievances?'

'Making my bed. School dinner. The French teacher. Getting up. Er—Latin. The way the bathroom door won't shut properly.'

'Some of those will clear up with the passage of time. The bathroom door has been like that for twenty years: one learns to live with it.'

'I wonder,' said Clare, 'if this house will be here when I'm old. If I'll live in it.'

'I don't imagine so for a moment. The whole place will have been razed to the ground to make way for a housing estate.'

'Maybe not,' said Aunt Anne. 'You never know. The road may come to be considered highly desirable. Preserved for posterity.'

'Either way, you won't need it. You will have furnished your own life, with other places and other things.'

'I shall keep the photographs from the drawing-room,' said Clare, 'and the clothes in the trunks in the attic, and the portraits in the dining-room, and ...'

'My dear child,' said Aunt Susan, 'you can't carry a museum round with you. Neither will you need to. What you need, you will find you already have to hand—of that I've not the slightest doubt. You are a listener. It is only those who have never listened who find themselves in trouble eventually.'

'Why?'

'Because it is extremely dull,' said Aunt Susan tartly, 'to grow old with nothing inside your head but your own voice. Tedious, to put it mildly.'

The fire heaved, flared up for a moment, and settled itself again. The logs hissed. Outside, a car went past. How odd, Clare thought, to sit here talking about me as though I were another person. Someone quite different. She tried to project herself forwards in time to meet her, this unknown woman with her name and her face, and failed. She walked away, the woman, a stranger, familiar and yet unreachable. The only thing you could know about her for certain was that all this would be part of her: this room, this conversation, the aunts.

The aunts. Aunt Anne, seventy-eight: Aunt Susan, eighty-one. I can't make it stop at now, Clare thought, and you shouldn't want to, not really.

She looked at them, intently, at their faces and their hands and the shape of them. I'm learning them by heart, she thought, that's what I'm doing, that's all I can do, only that.

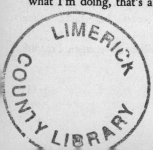